Windsinger

Frances Gillmor

with an introduction by the author

Foreword by N. Scott Momaday

A Zia Book

UNIVERSITY OF NEW MEXICO PRESS
Albuquerque

FOREWORD

On the dust jacket of the first edition of *Windsinger,*
published in 1930 by Minton, Balch & Company of
New York, Frances Gillmor is quoted as saying: "I
have spent considerable time on the Navajo reservation, far from railways and travelled roads. There I
have been able to see much of the life of the Navajo
hogans. I have travelled horseback at the foot of Black
Mesa, where in my story Windsinger lives, I have seen
sand painting in the making, a very rare privilege for
a white person, and something which women, either
white or Navajo, are seldom allowed to do. I have
been to chants and Entahs where I have been the only
white person present, and where in the strange
dramatic serenity of the firelit ceremonies of song, I
could easily forget that I myself was not a Navajo."

This statement—bear in mind that it was made
almost fifty years ago—gives us a keen insight into this
novel and this novelist, I believe. At first glance the
statement seems ordinary enough, the conventional
declaration of authority, the catalog of credentials
that leads her publisher to claim, somewhat exces-
sively, of course, that ". . . she has distilled the
essence of the Navajo. . . ." But there is something
rather more important than this in Frances Gillmor's
statement. There is a kind of rhetorical force which is
most like longing, a genuine respect for the particular

world of which she writes. In her final sentence, especially, there is a whole equation of love and wonder and delight.

It is this equation, too, that informs the whole narrative of the novel and that is responsible for *Windsinger*'s appeal now, as it was in 1930. Indeed, that appeal seems even a little more urgent in our time, as the world of the book's pages recedes into history.

The deep heart of the Navajo reservation was in some ways more remote from us in 1930 than it is in 1976. The reservation has changed: it is no longer the place where Frances Gillmor saw "much of the life of the Navajo hogans," nor is it so inaccessible to us as it was to the readers of *Windsinger* in 1930. The fact is, there are very few glimpses of that earlier world in our imaginative literature, for the reason that there were in those days very few persons who could or cared to write about the Navajos in novels. One thinks immediately of *Laughing Boy* (1929), by Oliver La Farge, and though that work is more novelistic, more literary, perhaps, on the surface, it is not necessarily truer in its evocation of the spirit of the Navajo people and their sacred ground.

The landscape is vivid and vital in *Windsinger,* and it is true, true to my own childhood experience of the Navajo reservation in the thirties and forties. There is some deep spiritual correlation there between man and the landscape, and that correlation is remarked with subtle beauty and insistence in Frances Gillmor's narrative. Consider this paragraph, for example:

Through the afternoon they followed the trail as it crossed and recrossed the wash. Water and quicksand did not hold them back. When they reached a stretch of sheep-cropped turf they broke into a canter. Grass grew in that canyon between the red cliffs, and tall spruce, dark against the heights of rock. Wild roses bloomed there, and the fragrance of rain stayed with them as they rode.

Or this:

The rain came again, cold on the gusty wind; rain plunging earthward, cold and hard. With each crack of thunder a blade of lightning cut the dark between him and the mesa. Again and again the horse turned his back to the wind and rain and blinding light. Still Windsinger urged him forward.

The prose here seems to me very straight and deliberate. And it seems also vivid and strong. Its strength proceeds from the sense of place, I believe, and the sense is whole and certain. In *Windsinger* we have a true evocation of a place that is wonderful in itself, written by one possessed of its wonder.

N. Scott Momaday
Stanford University
Stanford, California

AUTHOR'S INTRODUCTION

Toward midnight I was sitting in the brush cooking-shelter at a Navajo ceremony in Marsh Pass. I had heard no English all day except from the Navajo girl who had accompanied me to the ceremony. Now her mother was broiling some goat ribs for a late supper before we started back to Kayenta. We could hear the songs of healing being sung in the medicine hogan for her sister.

From the shadows beyond the glow of the piñon fire a girl's voice spoke in English.

"Are you the one who wrote *Windsinger?*" she asked.

A little worried, I admitted that I was. But I need not have worried. She said she had read it at school. She thought that it was good. This was the first time I had known of Navajos reading this book. The ordered ritual of the day just past, the hospitality of the host family, the friendliness of the moment in the firelit shelter were comfortable and good around me.

On a train in the East one day I was chatting with a stranger about the Navajo country. He remarked, "I was there some years ago when the strangest thing happened. Everyone started moving to the mesas because a man who had been struck by lightning said there would be a flood. Someone should write about that."

He was surprised to learn that someone had.

The event he remembered took place in 1922, and would have been remembered by many Navajos present at the ceremony in Marsh Pass. The traders talked about it, remembering the sound of the bells of sheep and goats, as the Navajos had passed in the night with their flocks on their way to higher ground.

From that event the novel *Windsinger* grew. It clothed itself in the Navajo colors of the four directions. It gathered to itself the mythical floods that had driven the people upward. It caught echoes from the myths of the beginning of rituals when a god sometimes came across the desert with a characteristic cry to a Navajo hunter or traveler, and later taught him the songs of a ceremony and the designs for a sand painting, drawing them with light on a cloud. So Windsinger finds his moment of illumination when there is no tension of seeking, and after rejection and disillusionment. It comes to him in quietness. It is given.

This book makes its statement in Navajo terms. But the statement could be made within many religious and philosophical contexts. The seeker could be anyone—a poet, a painter, a scientist—reaching for beauty, for truth.

Less dramatic use was made of the everyday events in Navajo life. I look at my early notes on Navajo country and am surprised by the hints of the book to come. I rode the mail truck into the reservation the first time—seventy-five miles and two days from Flagstaff to Kayenta over roads the Hopi driver often had to shovel out from drifting dune sand. Before we reached the reservation boundary we crossed an area where the water had failed and the homesteaders had left. My notes say: "One house stands there, one homesteader just moved in to make another attempt. Beside the road a dark-haired woman with anxious eyes and a little nervous laugh waits for her letters. The flat is loud with the shrilling of locusts." In the book I moved that woman into Navajo country. She was the one who could not make peace with the hard, wide land. I made her the wife of a farm agent who would have reason for being there and work to do for the land itself.

Short notations appear: "gulls and heron on the desert"; the coming and going in a trading post; what a mender of windmills said about the job he had held for twenty years, traveling from windmill to windmill with a Navajo boy for his helper, camping out at night, returning at intervals to his home to make parts for windmills on his blacksmith's anvil; a Navajo woman making a baby board; the view from under the great arch of Betatakin by day and by night.

From these roots the narrative grew. I am not sure that I knew how until the book was done, nor that I can now recreate the steps. But I think the book has truth as it stands, both in its particulars and in its symbolic statement.

Now automobiles speed along paved highways past motels owned and operated by the Navajo tribe, past oil and gas wells and sawmills. The annual tribal budget runs into millions of dollars. The steel towers of power lines march across the desert, resembling a row of ye'i in the sand paintings though they are not gods.

With the social stresses coming from increased movement and communication, people seek to understand each other across whatever boundaries may be—among them those between generations and between traditions. The effort is in both directions and, of course, is not new. Some years ago a pine tree was struck by lightning near a tuberculosis hospital then in existence in Tucson where most of the patients were Navajos. The director of the hospital sent at once to the Navajo country and had a singer flown south to conduct the proper chant through the intercom. More recently, with the foundation support and the participation of a psychiatrist in the project, a study group of young Navajos learned ceremonies from a number of old singers who taught the traditional chants in the traditional way in their own homes. The psychiatrist was reported as saying that he had learned much himself, and knew better when to refer his own patients to a singer.

In this era of increased sensitivity to a variety of cultural traditions, I hope that a new generation will read *Windsinger* and find it good, as the Navajo girl who spoke to me in a firelit hogan once did. I hope that readers on both sides of a boundary may find that they cross it as they read.

Frances Gillmor
1975

CONTENTS

I. THE WHITE WIND

From the east the white wind blew, the wind of a breaking day.

WINDSINGER

I

IN the night sounded the rise and fall of a chanted prayer and the voices of desert men singing. The cry rose from the hogan at the foot of the mesa and rose with the smoke to the windy sky; for a child was to be born to the People.

Toward the dim cliffs of the mesa drove the Mender of Windmills. The road was faint before him, and around him moonlight lay like snow upon the desert. Steadily he jogged along in the white night. The cliffs and the singing men came nearer. . . .

Up from the low land to the slope of piñon and cedar. . . . Up from the desert to the slope of the mesa. . . . The dim cliffs were near when the Mender of Windmills reached the Navajo fire.

They welcomed him there, and took his hand in a steady clasp of greeting. One moved in the firelight with a gleam of silver bracelets and belt.

"It is night, and the way has been long," he said to the Mender of Windmills. "Stay here until the day comes."

So it was that a white man that night spread his blanket beside the fire of the desert people and listened to the chanting men. There was prayer in the desert night, song in the desert silence. For a child was to be born.

The men smoked and talked as the fire burned low. They listened to the song which came from the hogan—now high, now low, now ending in an ejaculation which was more moan than song. They listened to the singers start again, and watched the flicker of the hogan fire between the crevices of logs and mud; and one slept, wrapped in his blanket.

At last the Mender of Windmills wrapped his blanket about him and slept also. The white moon climbed high above the cliffs. With no other light, the miles of desert stretched away to darkness.

※ ※

The sheep under the piñon trees stirred and were still, and the movement was like a wind touching the desert grass. From the hogan came the lift of song where men yet prayed and waited for a child to be born.

The chill of the night touched the sleeping men outside until one rose and put more wood on the dying coals. The silver clashing of bracelets sounded and then ceased as he once more settled himself to sleep. The chanting went on, the prayer and the pain, in the desert night. Then for a moment the song faded into silence and a woman's voice rose in a monotony of speech.

The men sleeping beside the fire awoke to listen. The Mender of Windmills turned in his blanket.

"An old woman speaks as one whose sight is keen," he was told. "She tells how the child lies; she tells when it will be born."

Her voice fell and ceased. Once more the chanting rose in the night. Once more pain and prayer and waiting.

The moon hung in the western sky when the men beside the fire woke again. In the hogan sounded a child's cry.

One of the singers lifted the blanket over the door and called,

"Hako—come!"

They crowded into the smoke filled interior. By the dim light of the coals they could see the mother lying on a sheepskin, the chief singer putting sacred objects into his medicine bag, the old women with the new born child in their midst.

"Ashki uzzi—ashki njoni" was the murmur. "A baby boy—a fine boy—"

The singers leaned against the log walls, smoking and resting. The firelight caught the gleam of silver, the purple and green and orange of velvet blouses, as the men and women came and went. An old woman left the hogan, and a moment later a young man entered, safe from the dark years of blindness which would be his if he looked upon the face of his wife's mother. He stood over his new born son, smiling.

"Yahteh, it is well."

Yahteh—the song and the prayer and the pain were stilled. The child was born. Voices and movement and laughter broke for a little while the silence of the desert.

More logs had been thrown upon the fire outside, and already the fragrance of coffee, and of tortillas cooking in fat, drew the hungry people. Two old women sat beside the fire, throwing the great disks of dough from arm to arm. A horse neighed in the shadow. The sheep stirred again like wind under the piñon trees.

※ ※

Suddenly the voices were hushed. An old man pointed to the sky.

"Olja, the moon!"

Murmuring, the desert people looked into the wide sky and saw that the white moon's edge was dimmed.

As they watched it, the murmur died to silence. A woman left the group by the fire, and lifting the blanket over the hogan door called the others to look. They stood there without words, until they saw that more and more of the moon would be darkened.

"The moon has fainted," said the old singer.

"The moon has fainted," agreed the young men.

Now where there had been rejoicing there was silence. For a child had been born, and must die.

"It is an eclipse," explained the Mender of Windmills. "A shadow—"

But they were not listening.

The shadow crept on across the face of the moon. Slowly the white disk turned to copper red. Slowly the white light upon the desert was shut out. The night was dark.

The Mender of Windmills heard the thud of saddles flung upon horses' backs, the quick trot of horses' feet as the people rode away through the night. They were going home . . . riding swiftly and in silence. . . .

Knowing only that fear had touched the people of the hogan the Mender of Windmills settled himself once more to sleep. But the singer and the father of the new born child talked earnestly beside the coals of the fire. The singer pointed at the copper disk that hung in the western sky. The father's face, stern in the dim light, refused to grant the thing that must be. At last the slow speech of the singer stopped. The father spoke his consent.

"The moon has fainted. The child must die."

The Mender of Windmills caught the phrase. He flung his blanket aside as they started toward the hogan.

"Stop," he cried. "The moon has not fainted. It is a shadow. . . ."

But again they paid no heed. They lifted the blanket over the door and entered the silent hogan. The Mender of Windmills followed them.

The fire had gone down to a heap of coals, already pale with ash. The mother was asleep on her sheepskin, and the old women sat silent in the shadow.

One stirred, and at the singer's question motioned toward the child lying beside her. This child of their clan still lived, though they knew he must die.

"There is no cause for death here," protested the Mender of Windmills. "Though no child had been born, the moon would be dark tonight. Not because of the child did this shadow come upon the moon."

The father of the child turned to him, stern with sorrow.

"Always the women must smother the child that is born when the moon faints. It was so of old, and still is so."

The Mender of Windmills was silent. Then once more he spoke.

"When must this thing be?"

"Before the white face of the moon shows again," came the slow answer from the singer, "the child must die."

The Mender of Windmills lifted the blanket and stepped outside.

"Come," he called. "The shadow is still on the moon. We have time for speech."

The old singer and the father of the child followed him out of doors. An old woman joined them a moment later. Darkened still with the red shadow of the earth, the moon hung above the desert. Copper red in the wide starred sky. A dark moon in the darkened night.

"The children of my people are not slain when a shadow comes upon the moon," said the Mender of Windmills. "The sun itself may hide its face, but a child that is born still lives, and no harm comes."

The old singer's wrinkled face was lifted to the copper moon.

"The knowledge of the white man is not like the knowledge of the men whom Old Age has slain among our people," he said. "The child must die. Since the beginning it has been so."

"The child must die," repeated the father sadly. "So it must be, although this morning I could see the smoke of my father's hogan afar off, and knew that it was a chindi hogan, burning because he was dead. So it must be, although twice, since last the sun rose, the breath of my family will have fled and left no trail. . . ."

The slow speech stopped. The Mender of Windmills stood by the fire watching with them the red moon of death. Already a thin white edge was pushing out from the copper shadow. The neighing of a horse, the movement of a sheep, the harsh voice of a burro afar off came with a swift sense of life into the silence.

"I have been told by your old men that each day one of your people must die," said the Mender of Windmills. "One each day. But this day, my friend, you tell me yourself that the life has been paid. Your father's breath has fled. Your son may live."

The strip of light widened at the edge of the copper shadow. Pale light lay upon the desert.

There was a new and quiet breathing of the wide night. . . .

"More than one life need not be paid," repeated the Mender of Windmills earnestly. "Even if the shadow on the moon should mean another death, let it not mean the death of this child. For when this child was born, the moon was white above the desert. Perhaps later another child was born—yonder across the mesa—perhaps because of that child the moon fainted. But I myself saw your son in this hogan before the moon was darkened."

"It is so," said the old woman slowly, peering at the Mender of Windmills through the dark. "The mother had been allowed to lie down upon her sheepskin; this child of our clan was born before the moon fainted."

"It is so," agreed the singer. "Though the moon fainted so quickly afterward, the child was born while the moon was white."

White light came again to the desert, stronger and clearer moment by moment. The Mender of Windmills was silent. If he had failed there was still the pinto pony to ride bare backed through the night. On the pinto pony with a child in his arms. . . . In the white night he waited.

The child's father spoke.

"The child was born while the moon was white.

This day my father's breath has fled, but this new breath shall not be smothered. The child shall live."

"It is well," said the singer. "The child shall live."

The old woman lifted the blanket at the door of the hogan. Through the smokehole the stars shone in the pale night sky. The old women still sat in the shadow, waiting.

"It is well," she told them. "This son of our clan shall not die. The child shall live."

The copper shadow was gone from the face of the moon. Low in the west white light shone upon the desert. But already in the east spread the pallor of dawn. From the mountains at the edge of the desert world the white wind blew—the wind of a breaking day.

The door of the trading post stood open to the sunlit distances. Two men clad in velvet blouses and belted with silver sat on a pile of wool and watched the wagon of the Mender of Windmills jolt away over the desert road.

"It is an evil thing that the child lives," said one.

"Evil or good—who knows? The gods have ever loved the scorned ones."

The half-breed trader behind the counter nodded.

"It is so," he agreed. "He who flew with the eagles through the sky; he who went down the Old Age Water; the twins crippled and blind—always it has been so. Perhaps this child also will go to the hogans of the gods and bring back songs to the People."

They smoked awhile in silence. A woman rode up to the door and dismounted. With soft moccasined tread she brought in three goatskins and laid them on the counter. When the trader had weighed them and counted out her money, she sat down on the mud floor, her striped skirt spread about her.

Outside the door the wind lifted a spiral of dust. They could hear the sibilant scraping as it moved away in the sunlight. The wheel of the windmill creaked.

"There will be sorrow in that hogan," prophesied the first man again. He rose as he spoke and stood for a moment in the door. The sun shone on his bright headband and on his long black hair knotted at the back. "The wisdom of the old men is forgotten."

He mounted his horse and rode off in the desert.

"There is new wisdom," said the trader. "They say a farmer comes here to show us how to grow corn like the Hopis."

"Let the Hopis have their corn," said the other. "The flocks of the desert belong to the women of the People."

Again silence fell upon them. A colt stuck his head curiously into the door. At a slow command from the seated woman the trader cut a length of purple velvet.

Outside the hogan where the new born boy was lying, an old woman sat by the fire fashioning a baby board. She marked the holes with charcoal from the fire, and burned them through with wire heated in the coals. Within the hogan the mother of the child lay on her sheepskin looking east to the far blue mountains.

As the old woman worked, she was singing. Her song told of the first baby board which the gods had made—a baby board whose back and foot rest were made of sunbeams, whose hood was made of rainbow, whose lacings were of zigzag lightning.

Noon high the sun blazed upon the hogan, and picked out the silver studdings of a saddle flung over the bough of a piñon tree. The wind breathed in the crannies of the rocks. Above them was the height of the mesa, dark as if the shadow of a cloud were on it.

II

DAYS of wind and sun and sand; days when shreds of distant rain curtained the mountains; and always over the desert the flocks of the People drifted. . . .

The half-breed looked out of the trading post at the sheep and goats moving slowly by. A little herdboy followed them, keeping an eye on the strays and turning them back to the flock, waiting while they drank from the trough at the foot of the windmill. Around him moved the sheep, black and white and red, whose wool would be sold to the trader or carded and spun and woven in his mother's hogan; the goats also, whose hides would be brought some day to the trading post.

A white man stood beside the trader and watched them drink.

"Whose sheep are these?" he asked.

The trader answered the farmer slowly.

"They belong to the wife of the Man Who Rides a Black Horse." He paused and added, "At this boy's birth the moon fainted."

The sheep and the goats were already moving on. With the tinkling of little bells they passed the only other house in the settlement, and in the yard the farmer's wife looked up from an iron pot. She brushed the faded hair from her forehead with the back of her hand and stood looking after them. When their bells and low cries were lost in the distances she still stood looking out to the far meeting place of desert and sky. At last she turned again, and prodded the boiling clothes. . . .

The little sheep herder took shelter from the noonday sun under a piñon tree. Around him the sheep and goats nibbled at the dry grass. Save for them there was no sound in the desert silence. In the shade the little sheep herder played with the sand, letting it fall from his hand in thin sure lines as he had seen the singers do when they made a sand painting. But in his hand he held no dull rich blue, nor red like the sand of the singers; only tawny gold like the sun-gold distances, stretching away to the cliffs of the mesa dimmed with noon. Drowsily the boy watched his flock. Quick to notice the red sheep which had strayed, he flung a stone beyond it and turned it back to the others. Sun and wind-gold distances and the mesa looking always as if the shadow of a cloud were on it. . . . At last the little sheep herder left his place of cool shade and started his flock again on its slow nibbling way. He was singing under the desert sun. . . .

There was death in the hogans of the People. It had come on the wind that swept cold from the mountain snows. It had come on the snow that lay at last upon the desert itself. As the Mender of Windmills made his slow way from mill to mill there were many who came to him with a tale of fever and struggling breath and stillness at the end. He turned aside with them; and many a grave he dug on the windy slopes of the mesa, or beneath the shadow of El Capitan, that towering shaft of basalt that the People call Agathla, the place of the scraping of hides.

Beyond Agathla smoke rose from the desert places between the buttes, and the Mender of Windmills, watching, knew that there too death had been, and the hogans of the dead were burning.

※ ※

Down from the slope of the mesa rode a woman and a boy. They were astride a black horse, but they went slowly, driving the sheep before them. Behind them rose a column of smoke. Silent and dark it rose from the hogan of the Man Who Rode a Black Horse. And his wife and son rode the horse away.

Down from the slope of the mesa, on across the white floor of the desert. . . . No need now to follow the trails to the windmills, for the sheep could lick the snow. The woman wrapped her blanket more closely about her.

"We will find others of our clan," she said to her son. "We will go to the hogans beyond Agathla and find our kinsmen there."

They turned and looked back toward the cliffs of the mesa. At the foot of the cliff they had buried the Man Who Rode a Black Horse, buried him with all his silver and coral and turquoise that he might go unashamed to his fathers. Smoke rose from the hogan which they had fired, obedient to a command given long ago to the People, when the wind whispered in the ear of one bereaved, saying,

"Go not back into the hogan. You have had sorrow there."

They watched the distant smoke. Then with their flock moving before them they set their faces northward toward the pinnacle of Agathla.

彎 彎

North of Agathla two Mormons on a day of gray wind and snow came upon a flock of sheep and goats huddled together in the shelter of some high rocks. They saw no hogan near, nor any herder with them, until through the storm they saw a small figure lying wrapped in a blanket among the sheep.

As the two men came near, the sheep scattered

and stood watching curiously from a little distance. The blanket was flung aside, and a little boy supported himself on one elbow and flung a stone to turn them back. When he saw the two men he wrapped his blanket about him again, and only his two frightened eyes looked forth at them.

"Get up, kid," said one of them kindly. "You'll freeze to death there."

The boy looked at him uncomprehendingly.

"He's all right," said the other. "He'll stay out the storm here and when it's over take his bunch of sheep home safe. They're good herders, these kids."

They pulled their horses around and started away. Then at the sound of the boy's voice they drew up. He had let the blanket fall from his head and was looking after them.

"What's that? Talk American!"

He looked at them with a frightened and pleading expression. In the slow speech of the desert people he spoke again.

One of the men shook his head.

"We don't get you, kid. No savvy."

As they started away once more, the boy struggled to his feet and took a step or two toward them. Then he fell.

"Hell, Jim. The kid's sick—"

He swung down from his saddle and bent over the little sheep herder.

"He's got a fever—"

The boy sat up once more and, pointing, spoke again in his own lauguage.

The man on horseback followed his pointing finger. He could see nothing through the snow.

"But it's something about his mother, Bill," he said. "Shimah—mother."

"He wants us to get his mother and tell her he's sick," guessed Bill. "There's a hogan near here like as not."

"We can't leave him here or he'll be dead right now," said Jim. "Come on, Jim, swing him up here and we'll take him to his hogan. I guess we can drive this bunch of sheep along with us."

But, as they lifted him, he beat them away weakly with his fists.

The two men paused in perplexity. He watched them again in frightened silence. The wind cried above them among the rocks.

Jim swung into his saddle.

"We'll have to get his mother," he said. "It's all right, kid. We'll get your mother. Understand? Your mother—shimah."

"Shimah," nodded the boy, and pointed again.

They rode off, the horses picking their way over

sand and snow. A few sheep, strayed from the others, watched them from a sheltered place among the rocks. Suddenly Jim pulled up his horse, and peered ahead.

"What's that?" he exclaimed.

Again they swung down from their saddles and bent over a blanketed figure. But here there was no sound nor movement. When they lifted a corner of the blanket they saw a woman, dead.

They stood silently while the snow fell from the gray clouds. Above them red rocks were pitched like gigantic hogans against the sky. And there the high rock wind was crying still. . . .

Nearby they found a black horse tied to a cedar. His saddle had been thrown over the crutch of the tree, and beneath the tree was a flour sack containing a spindle, a carder, and an iron pot.

"They were moving, Jim—the kid and his mother. They were taking their sheep and all their belongings—"

"Look around. Perhaps we'll find some more of the family."

At last they came back to the woman who lay dead in the snow.

"There's no shovel to dig a grave—"

"And there's no hogan in sight."

The two men looked out across the distance. To

the north the buttes of Monument Valley showed dimly. To the south El Capitan rose against the sky. No smoke of a fire nor shape of a hogan was visible on the snowy waste.

"There's just one thing to do, Jim. We'll carry her up into a crevice of the rocks, and pile rocks over the entrance to keep the coyotes away."

Together they carried the blanketed figure up into the rocks. Together they lifted the boulders for her burial. There among the rocks, with the wind and snow driving across the desert, they left the wife of the Man Who Rode a Black Horse.

The boy's feverish eyes watched them as they talked of what could be done for him. They had left the black horse tied near by. They had explained to the boy with gestures that they had found his mother and built her a tomb among the high rocks. It had seemed to them that silent as he was he had understood and been comforted. But now they looked at him in perplexity.

"I tell you, Jim, it ain't right to leave him here." The wind reddened face was troubled.

"But it ain't right to bring the disease to town."

They looked at the dark eyes peering at them from beneath the blanket. They looked at the wide space of snow and wintry sky.

Bill rubbed his roughened cheek.

"But he might die here—like the squaw—"

"The kids at home might die, Bill. With a quarantine on the reservation we can't bring him back, and him sick too."

Above them the wind moved among the rocks. The sheep huddled closer to the base of the ridge.

"We can leave him food, and maybe we'll find a hogan on our way home and send someone back for him. That's all we can do, Bill."

So it was decided at last. They brought wood and piled it near him, enough to last the night through. They built a fire.

"When the wood's gone, he can curl up with the sheep and keep warm like he was when we found him," said Jim reassuringly.

Before they rode away Bill unstrapped another blanket from behind his saddle. As he tucked it around the boy, he could feel him shivering.

"I don't like it, Jim. If it was a white kid we wouldn't leave him like this."

But at last they rode off together. The little sheep herder, without speaking, watched them go. Only his dark eyes looked out from his blanket. He rolled a little nearer the fire which they had left. Above him the wind sounded between the rocks, and still the snow fell. . . . After a little while the sheep came near again.

The Mormon bishop looked at the two men before him.

"So you left him there," he said thoughtfully.

His brow wrinkled with his slow stern thinking. He was more used to labor under the sun, making green acres in the desert. . . .

"It wasn't right to leave him," he said at last.

The two men looked worried.

"We did the best we knowed how," pleaded Jim. "We didn't want this here epidemic to hit the town."

"And we left him food, and a blanket," added Bill.

The bishop shook his head.

"It wasn't right. It was better that the whole town should die."

He grew red faced with his slow tide of feeling.

"Go back," he ordered, "Find the boy. Bring him here."

Down the street of bare cottonwoods and forth into the desert they rode again, between the buttes of Monument Valley to the ridge of red rocks pitched like hogans against the sky. But though they found the rock tomb of the woman they had buried, they found no trace of the boy and his sheep.

"His people found him, likely enough," they decided.

And they rode back again to the Mormon town and the street of bare cottonwoods.

❧ ❧

The way was long beyond Agathla. Through cold dawns the flock moved on, followed by the little sheep herder on his black horse. When the sun was high there was warmth in the sheltered places among the rocks, and there the boy slept for a little while and felt strength flow into him again. Then on between great heights of rock where the buttes arose under the light filled day, on toward the hogans of his people he moved until dark fell. Even then the winter moon lighted his way, until through weariness he stopped, and lying among the sheep found warmth enough to sleep for a little while.

Lying so he buried his face one night in the rough wool and shook with hard sobs. He wept in loneliness, knowing that nowhere on the desert was his mother in a hogan, weaving as she waited for him to come home with the sheep. Nowhere a hogan fire burned with his father beside it telling tales in the long night. Only somewhere ahead were the hogans of his clan, the unknown hogans of his mother's people. . . . The wind cried across the desert from the far cliffs of the mesa, cried among the heights of rock that were dark against the sky. . . . At last the boy's hot tears ceased, and he slept with the warmth of the sheep's bodies against his. In the morning he went on again, riding his black horse and driving the sheep before him.

The day came when the food which the white men had given him was gone. On that day he killed one of the sheep in his flock, killed it as he had seen his mother do when there was to be a great feast in the hogan at the foot of the cliffs. Now, so long had he seen no other living thing, he waited, half expecting the sheep to speak in protest, as to a friend to whom for many days it had been kind. Indeed the tales the old men told were of animals speaking with the voices of gods. . . . But no voice came in the sunlit morning. When he had killed the sheep, he made a fire, striking sparks with flint upon the dry grass he had been able to gather among the rocks. He took the iron pot from the flour bag, and set the mutton to boil in melted snow. When he had eaten his fill he took as much with him as he could carry and went on.

No flocks crossed his path over the desert, and no hogans sent up smoke to the cold sky. The way was long beyond Agathla. . . .

One evening as the sun lighted the heights of

red rock, the boy saw a hogan. Smoke was rising there and he knew that he would find people. His own people perhaps, men of his blood and clan who would welcome him. In the early dark he brought his sheep to that hogan. There he ate bread baked of piñon nuts, and corn parched and cooked in the ashes. He slept all night on sheepskins beside the fire. But the people there were not of his clan. In the morning they pointed the way to the hogans of his mother's people and he went on.

Another sun rose and set before he reached the end of his journey. There at last he found welcome and rest. His flocks were added to his grandmother's, and in the days that followed he was content to tend them and to come back at the end of day to the hogan where, until the light failed, she sat before her loom weaving.

She told him the tales of their clan—how long ago the People wandering in the desert saw fires afar off and how there they found men like themselves. She told him of the night he himself was born, and how on that night the moon fainted. Through the long days the boy thought of these things.

Sometimes others of their family would come riding from their hogans, and they looked with interest at the boy of whose birth they had heard.

Straight was his body under the ragged velvet blouse. His hair, tied with a red silk band, was long. And his eyes seemed ever to search the far edge of the desert and the heights of red rock.

"Surely it is well that this boy lived," they said. "The gods could not have hated him at his birth."

Then over the desert they would ride to their own hogans leaving the two alone once more, the grandmother, wrinkled and lean and old, weaving bright blankets on her loom, the boy herding his sheep under the winter sun.

≥⋲ ⋲≥

Still there was death in the hogans of the People —death and song on the desert.

The little sheep herder watched the men make prayer sticks of juniper and sage, of cornshucks and cat-tails. Placed in front of the hogan as sacrifices to the gods, perhaps they would bring help and healing. . . .

He watched the men make the sand painting. Bright and sure the lines of sand fell from their fingers and the design grew—corn and beans and squash and tobacco, and stars against the night sky. The singer gave brief directions— "Blue." "Yellow." "Black." As the men worked the sunlight fell through the smokehole, and touched to brighter colors the headbands and the sand painting.

In the afternoon the little herdboy watched his sick grandmother as, led by the singer, she came into the hogan and sat on the sand painting. He listened to the chanting while the sun sank lower and lower in the western sky. Before the sun was set they led his grandmother away and rubbed the sand painting out. With all things done according to the wisdom of the old men and the command of the gods, surely there would be healing. . . .

At night while the firelight flared and died the herdboy listened to the chanting again, as the old men sang to the beat of rattles and drums. Sheep from the flocks went to the singers. At noon and at night the women were cooking for those who had come to add their voices to the chanted rites.

But still there was death in the hogans of the People.

光光

The late weeks of winter came, and none was left of the little sheep herder's family. In ragged velvet he tended his flock, and when the day was over he went back to a hogan where they told him the flock was not his.

"Who has heard of a boy with sheep?" they asked him scornfully. "Who would not laugh to hear you? The sheep belong to us; for we give you shelter as if you were our own."

But these women did not send their own children to herd sheep from daybreak to dark. Through the long days the son of the Man Who Rode a Black Horse wandered with the flock in search of grass, and when night came he was given food grudgingly.

"Here is corn, greedy one. Take it and begone."

Away from the fire he sat in the shadow eating his handful of parched corn. He learned to be silent; for the man with the crooked mouth who lounged in the sun all day was quick to anger, and his wives were sharp-tongued. When one rode away to the distant trading post carrying goatskins behind her saddle, the other spoke ill of her to their husband; and when he spoke kindly to one, the other let her wrath fall upon the little sheep herder.

"Now truly misfortune comes to the hogan where you dwell. Better that you had been killed the night of your birth. Better that you go out on the desert to find a bed among the rocks and eat gophers for your food."

Only on the desert with his flock did he find quietness. While the sheep grazed, the little herdboy thought of the stories his grandmother had told him, thought of his own birth and his own destiny.

"The gods have walked with me," he decided.

"They remembered me at my birth, and surely not with hatred or they could have killed me long ago. Sickness came to my people, and I alone lived. Storm and cold and great distances lay between me and the hogans of my mother's kinsmen, but I came safely all the way. Since my birth the gods have walked with me."

After thinking of these things he carried himself with new dignity when he came back to the hogan of Crooked Mouth. When the women spoke to him in sharp scorn, he did not cringe, neither did he seem to hear them.

"Perhaps the gods may speak to me," he thought sometimes. "They may speak to me as they have spoken to others, at dawn when I awake, or on the desert when I am alone."

In the early morning while the others were still sleeping he lay waiting for the call of the talking god of dawn to sound four times on the desert, for a shuffling moccasined tread at the hogan door.

Spring came at last to the desert, and still the little herdboy dwelt in the hogan of Crooked Mouth. But a plan was slowly coming to shape as he wandered with his sheep, a plan for flight and freedom.

"Should I, who walk with gods, live like a Paiute slave?" he asked himself. "I will go back through

the valley of great rocks, past the place of the
scraping of hides, until I come again to the cliffs
of the mesa."

For a long time he thought of the sheep. He
knew that Crooked Mouth and his wives would be
glad enough to see him go. But if he took the sheep,
what then? Along their broad trail Crooked Mouth
and his wives would come riding. They would turn
the sheep back, and if he went on, he would go on
alone. Then he would go alone from the first.
Alone, taking not even the black horse his father
rode. For Crooked Mouth rode the black horse
now. . . .

The boy thought bitterly of that. Perhaps when
he found again men whom he could trust he would
tell them of the sheep and of the black horse. He
might even appeal to the white man's justice, to
the farmer whom the People of the desert trusted,
or to the Mender of Windmills whose voice had
already been raised on behalf of the son of the Man
Who Rode a Black Horse. The farmer or the
Mender of Windmills would help him.

But all this belonged to the future. Now he
could only plan his flight. He put away a little
food for his journey. And one night when the
people of the hogan were asleep he went out into
the desert.

Across the desert came the Mender of Windmills. At first he was a slow moving dust beyond the pinnacle of Agathla—a dust from which pale spirals rose now and then and marched alone across the slope, a dust which came slowly nearer and nearer until the boy on the rocks could see the jolting wagon and the man who held the reins.

He looked as if he might be sleeping as his horse jogged along. But occasionally his eyes swept the height of rock against the noon sky, and the far miles of desert under the noon sun.

No longer were there snowdrifts for the thirsty flocks of the People. Now only this hot wind, burning up the grass, drying up the waterholes. And here and there on the parched surface of the earth, silver wheels turning in the wind. . . .

Silver wheels that must not cease to turn . . . troughs beneath them that must not fail. . . . The Mender of Windmills slapped the reins on the back of his pinto pony.

The boy watched him come nearer and finally clambered down from the rocks and stood waiting by the side of the road. His velvet blouse was torn and dirty and his feet were bare. But he showed no shyness nor fear as he waited, head high, for the white man to stop. When the Mender of Windmills pulled up beside him, they looked at each other gravely, the boy of the People, and the still youthful mender of the People's windmills. Gravely too they shook hands. Then after the manner of the desert they were silent.

"Where do you go?" asked the boy at last.

The Mender of Windmills pointed ahead. In the distance were the cloud blue cliffs of the mesa.

"I go to the silver wheel that turns where the ridge of red rock meets the desert," he replied. "And then I go farther to the cliffs of the mesa."

"I go also this road," said the boy.

Together they rode on under the hot noon. An eagle drifted against the copper flame of the sky. On the desert they alone seemed to move in blazing windy light. . . .

The Mender of Windmills listened to the slow speech of the boy beside him. He knew him now for the child whose life he had saved when the moon fainted. With his eyes half shut against the sun and sand he heard for the first time that those with whom he had pleaded for the child's life had all fallen before the plague of the winter. The Man Who Rode a Black Horse, the old woman who had stood with them as they watched the red shadow on the moon, the mother sleeping on her sheepskin bed, the grandmother tending the newborn child—all these were again dust of the desert. Only he and the child still moved under the sun. . . .

Slowly the boy beside him told the story of the winter. For long intervals they were silent as they jolted along, dipping now into dry arroyos, climbing now the slopes of sun. Much the Mender of Windmills had to guess of the cold nights when the boy slept among his sheep for warmth, of the weary miles when ill and hungry he pushed on toward the hogans of his clan. But bit by bit the story was told. The Mender of Windmills heard at last of the bitter refuge the boy had found in the hogan of Crooked Mouth, and of his flight into the desert leaving the sheep behind.

At last the boy fell silent. They had left the height of Agathla behind. Now they reached a wash and waited for the pinto pony to drink. It would take a rain in the canyons to fill the wash bank-high with a roaring brown torrent; a rain which would bring water to the dry stream beds, and green to the desert. They forded the wash and went on.

Not until then did the Mender of Windmills speak a guarded word of encouragement.

"The sheep are yours," he said to the boy beside him. "Perhaps the farmer will tell us how to deal with Crooked Mouth."

With this the boy was content; the Mender of Windmills was his friend.

Up from the wash they drove, skirting the ridge of red rock until the windmill was suddenly within sight. Beyond the windmill was the half-breed's trading post, and a short distance away, the farmer's house. A dog barked as they approached, and a little girl clad like her elders in a bright velvet blouse and a long striped skirt came to the door of the trading post and watched them curiously. In the loneliness of wind and sun there was a sudden sense of movement and life.

The Mender of Windmills pulled up beside the trough. Here at the meeting place of the desert trails, the ground was beaten by the feet of sheep and goats, of cattle and horses. Even now a little girl on a burro was bringing her flock to drink.

The Mender of Windmills reflected with satisfaction that this water did not eat holes in the water column nor leave a deposit to cut the leather valves. Dependable and sure, this windmill gave its water to the desert people.

The boy wandered off to the trading post where perhaps he would find friends of his people and his clan. Around the Mender of Windmills the small cries of the sheep sounded; above him was the hum of the whirling silver wheel.

While he worked, the farmer trotted up to the windmill on horseback.

"You'll come up and take pot luck with us when you're done," the farmer urged.

The Mender of Windmills shook his head.

"Not tonight. It'll be beans and coffee out toward the mesa for me. I've got to make time this trip."

The farmer laughed.

"You're turning into a white man again, are you? What's your hurry?"

The Mender of Windmills smiled slowly.

"I'm trying to get ahead of a Navajo," he said. "And I've got to travel to do it. I've got to talk to you about it too."

"Then you'd better come up to supper. The wife'll be glad to have some company. She's near crazy with lonesomeness."

"Is she now! That's too bad." The Mender of Windmill's face showed quick and kindly concern. "It's a hard country for a woman, sure enough."

The older man grunted doubtfully.

"Country's all right. She says she'd give five years of her life to see green marshes again. But a few years and she'll see green corn fields and irrigation dams here that'll beat anything she's seen down south."

The Mender of Windmills was putting his tools back into his cart.

"If she's homesick a field of corn won't cure her," he said briefly. "I don't know as seeing people will either."

"Seeing you'll give her something to think about," protested the farmer. "And you can tell me about the Navajo you're after. Better come! Save your beans and coffee for tomorrow."

The Mender of Windmills nodded.

"I'll come," he agreed. "Thanks."

But the Mender of Windmills did not seek the fenced yard of the farmer until he had gone first to the trading post. He sat on a pile of wool and smoked while he listened to the talk. The half-breed and the two or three men lounging beside him were discussing the boy at whose birth the moon fainted. They talked too of Crooked Mouth. Now and then the Mender of Windmills put a question to them. At last he shook the tobacco from his pipe and went out.

The sun was going down, and to the west the black edge of a mesa cut the gold of the sky. The full moon was rising in the east, its great disk flushed with red. In the sunset there was suddenly a thin high note of song. The Mender of Windmills saw ahead of him a flock of sheep and goats and the little Navajo herdgirl singing as she drove them home.

For a minute she paused to watch him put the nose bag on his pinto pony. Then as he walked up the hill to the farmer's, he heard her again, singing in the dusk.

The farmer's wife came to the kitchen door to greet him.

"It's good to see you," she said earnestly. "Come in. I'm just dishing up."

She moved anxiously about the kitchen.

"We'd have bought a sheep from the Indians if we'd known you were coming," she told him. "It'll be just a pick-up dinner."

"It's a sight better than the beans and coffee I'd have alone, Mrs. Davison," said the Mender of Windmills. "It isn't often I sit down to a table with folks."

To his surprise he saw tears in her eyes as she looked at him.

"It's bad enough when you have a house and a place of your own," she said. "I don't see how you stand it."

He brushed aside her concern with a laugh.

"I was made to keep moving. I'm glad my job takes me off from the settled places."

"Don't you ever get lonesome?"

He laughed again.

"I get lonesome in towns."

She sighed as she looked out over the desert.

"I guess it's different with men—"

With a quick motion she went to the door.

"Come to supper, Henry."

The three sat down in the kitchen, and as the darkness deepened they ate the hearty supper of beans and potatoes and canned vegetables.

"We won't be eating canned vegetables much longer," boasted Davison. "We'll be having truck farms around here that'll give green stuff to the folks for fifty miles around. Why, this year you ought to see the corn and squash and melon up here by the dam."

He drew on the tablecloth maps of future irrigation ditches.

"Ten years from now this won't be desert at all," he declared.

"Ten years!" There was despair in his wife's voice.

A silence fell upon them. When they broke it, they spoke of other things.

The farmer's wife had poured more coffee and cut great slabs of pie for them when the Mender of Windmills spoke at last of the boy at whose birth the moon had fainted. He told them the story of the boy's long journey to the hogans of his mother's clan, and of his flight from the hogan of Crooked Mouth.

"But the sheep are his," he exclaimed. "He kept them together and herded them. It isn't right that he should lose them now."

"Poor little fellow," exclaimed the farmer's wife. "Think of him alone on the desert. . . ."

"It's too bad for him to lose the sheep," admitted the farmer. "He had pluck, that kid."

"He'll lose them unless someone can scare Crooked Mouth into giving them up."

"And you want to wish that job on me!" the farmer exclaimed.

"No, I'm taking on that job myself," declared the Mender of Windmills. "All I want is to know that you're back of me if they come to you as the big judge."

The farmer considered the matter cautiously.

"This boy's just one," he said. "There may be dozens in just as bad a fix. They died like flies this winter here on the reservation."

"We can see that this boy at least has what's due him," maintained the Mender of Windmills.

"But there'll be others claiming sheep from all their aunts and cousins. Who'll get at the right then?"

"No one'll claim sheep from the women of their own clan," promised the Mender of Windmills. "This is a case by itself—and they'll all know that."

The farmer looked doubtful as he shoved his pie plate away and stood up. They walked out into the yard and found seats on some rocks. The wind had gone down with the end of day, and the cool night was still. In the house the farmer's wife was clearing the table.

"Seems like you're going to a lot of trouble for this kid," insisted the farmer.

The Mender of Windmills chuckled.

"Sure. He sort of belongs to me. Didn't you know that?"

Then the Mender of Windmills told the farmer of that other white night, when the red shadow crept over the face of the moon and at the foot of the mesa the wisdom of the white man duelled with the wisdom of the red man for the fate of a new born child.

The farmer whistled.

"So that's it!"

"That's it," nodded the Mender of Windmills. "I've just naturally got to see that kid of mine get what's coming to him."

"I remember seeing him once with his flock,"

recalled the farmer. "Someone told me the moon had fainted when he was born."

"That's the boy," nodded the Mender of Windmills again.

They puffed contentedly on their pipes and for a little were silent.

"Then you'll back me up with Crooked Mouth?" asked the Mender of Windmills at last.

The farmer hesitated.

"It's like this, Matthew," he said to the Mender of Windmills. "I don't like to get mixed up in these people's quarrels. It's not my job—nor yours for that matter, though it's easy to see your side of it. When they bring a quarrel to me it's different. We're a long way from the agency, and it's up to me, I suppose, to be the judge. But most of the time they settle things themselves. It's better that way."

"Much better," agreed the Mender of Windmills heartily. "But this is different. They won't settle this themselves."

"Not if the boy takes it to the old men?"

"Not then." The Mender of Windmills paused. "He'll get no help from his own people."

"Then there's something to say for Crooked Mouth?" asked the farmer quickly.

The Mender of Windmills shook his head.

"No, it's not because they're for Crooked Mouth.

I've been listening to them talk down here at the post. They're for the boy, all of them."

"Then let them fight his battles," urged the farmer.

"They won't," repeated the Mender of Windmills. "They're afraid of Crooked Mouth." He paused a moment, then added casually, "He practices witchcraft."

The farmer looked up quickly.

"Talk like a white man, Matthew."

"It's a fact," chuckled the Mender of Windmills. "Crooked Mouth looked at a sick woman once and said she'd die. Sure enough, she did. It wouldn't have been so bad if it had happened just once, but it happened again with another woman. Witchcraft? You just ask 'em."

The farmer considered this.

"Then why wouldn't they be glad to put something over on him?" he demanded.

"They would—but not when there's a death penalty attached. Why, Davison, he's played on their fear of him for years. He's got a big flock through it—not the flock he's grabbed from this youngster, but his own. If he goes to a Navajo woman and demands a sheep, or two or three, will she dare refuse him? Hardly!"

The farmer laughed.

"So you figure it's up to you to risk death for this youngster of yours."

"That's it. But joking aside, you get the idea now, don't you, that this kid needs a little white man's justice?"

The farmer put out his hand.

"Do your damndest, Matthew. I'm with you!"

The two men shook hands in the moonlight.

Before the Mender of Windmills left, he went again to the kitchen door.

"It's time I was drifting, Mrs. Davison," he said. "But I'll see you all next trip."

She came toward him, wiping her hands on her apron.

"Don't forget that," she urged him. "You've a place here to come to, you know."

As he strode down the hill to the trading post, she stood at the door watching him. When at last he drove away in the moonlight night with the boy beside him, he could see her still standing in the lighted doorway, looking out over the desert.

He told the boy something of his plan as they drove along. For a few days more they would travel the roads between the windmills; then together they would go to the country of the great rocks beyond Agathla, to the hogan of Crooked Mouth.

"It is well," said the boy.

The Mender of Windmills understood the relief and the gladness behind his words.

For a long while they drove in silence toward the pale cliffs of the mesa. Then the pinto pony broke into a trot. And in time to the trot the Mender of Windmills heard the boy beside him singing a low song.

They sat in the shade of the summer chao, and the green cedar boughs above them tempered the heat of noon. In from the desert the sheep were coming.

"I have spoken to you in peace," said the Mender of Windmills. "Rabbits and watermelon I brought to you for a feast; and three hours we have counselled together. It is enough."

"It is enough," agreed Crooked Mouth with a sly smile.

"Then I go now, and the boy with me. But we go driving before us the sheep that are his."

"How will you take them?" asked Crooked Mouth.

"Since words of peace have failed, I take them by power that I alone have," said the Mender of Windmills.

"Is the white man a god, that he, and he alone, has this power?"

"Not a god but a mender of windmills," was the reply. "I hold in my hand the water of the desert. I give it or withhold it as I will."

Crooked Mouth waited. The faces of the women were impassive.

"When your waterholes dry up, you will go to the turning silver wheel; and there you will find no water."

"The water beneath the silver wheel does not fail."

"It has not failed. That is true. But I have been your friend. Now when you take your sheep to the silver wheel, you will find the trough empty. When you go on to the next, there too your sheep will find no water. Will you lose the whole flock, or will you give this boy the sheep that belong to him and keep the sheep that belong to you?"

Around them were small cries and the ringing of little bells as the flock came to the shade of the cedars and piñons. The Mender of Windmills watched two children dismount from a black horse. In the chao there was silence.

"He threatens—and will forget," murmured one of the women.

"His power is less than his speech," said the other.

"Dead men cannot stop a silver wheel from turning," suggested Crooked Mouth.

The Mender of Windmills did not take his eyes from the black horse.

"Dead men cannot start a silver wheel that has ceased to turn," he said evenly. "And within a day's journey on a swift horse you will find no water in the windmill troughs. The water is shut off, and the pumps are broken."

Again there was silence in the chao.

"Then other flocks go thirsty," remarked Crooked Mouth.

"For three days the other flocks have been moving. Three days ago the warning went forth to all the sheep herders except your children, and they have taken their sheep away."

The women stirred. One called to the two children who had come in with the sheep, and now were watching the council in the chao.

"There was no water," they told her. "The trough at the windmill was empty."

Crooked Mouth's lips twisted angrily.

"This flock too can follow the others to water."

The Mender of Windmills nodded gravely.

"But where will you find grass for so many?" he asked calmly. "You are the last to go to the new grazing places."

"Where will the others find grass in a country where already there are flocks?"

The Mender of Windmills looked out over the desert.

"They have agreed to go, until this boy's sheep are driven by."

Again there was silence. Then Crooked Mouth spoke.

"Shall I go unrewarded for giving the boy food and shelter from the cold?"

"He will do justly," said the Mender of Windmills. "Ten sheep from his flock and yonder black horse shall be yours,—a good horse though he is old and you have ridden him hard."

Crooked Mouth considered this in silence. The Mender of Windmills waited.

At last the slow words came.

"Let him take his sheep and go."

"You have spoken as a wise man should," said the Mender of Windmills. "One thing only must you not forget. These sheep are his forever. If word comes to me that you have followed him to the place of his hogan, and taken his sheep away, then once more the silver wheel will bring no water."

"Let him take his sheep and go," repeated Crooked Mouth. "I do not follow."

Under the hot noon they divided the flocks.

When they were through, the Mender of Windmills and the boy at whose birth the moon fainted started forth on foot into the desert. Suddenly they heard the voice of Crooked Mouth.

"I do not follow. But the day will come when this boy will bring back the sheep and beg me to take them. His body is thin. I can see his bones. And I can see that already he sickens and will die."

The Mender of Windmills looked quickly at the boy beside him. But on the boy's face there was no fear. He turned back and faced the hogan of Crooked Mouth, a slight figure in ragged velvet under the desert noon. For the first time that morning he spoke.

"I live unafraid; for I walk with gods."

And in silence he and the Mender of Windmills drove the flock down from the slope of piñon to the level distances of sun.

※ ※

Again the boy came to the cliffs of the mesa. There through days of white light he tended his sheep, and, when the sun was low, brought them home again to the shade of the piñons.

He had found people of his own clan on his way back from the hogan of Crooked Mouth. They were living near a dam which the farmer had built.

"Stay with us," they said. "There is water here, and our cornfields are already green. When the summer is past we will go to the slope of the mesa

where there are piñon nuts to be gathered and wood
for the winter. Then you too may go with us."

But the boy would not stay with them.

"When the summer is over," he said, "I will be
watching for you. But now I go on alone."

There beneath the pale cliffs he had built a summer hogan of green boughs.

"They will help me raise stout logs when they
come," he planned. "I will build a hogan then for
the time of snow and wind."

But now the green boughs gave him shade, and
the boy was glad as he worked. He built the shelter
with song, and when it was done he sang the song
of dedication.

"For here there is no singer, and it is not good
to forget the gods who walk with me," he decided.

He sang again when he built his first fire, and
his song was a prayer that it might burn with
peace in that hogan. It was a woman's prayer—

"But here there is no woman to pray for the happiness of this place."

At evening when the sun was set he sat by his
fire content. Surely he still walked with gods.
Surely the god of the hogan, who was also god of
evening, would come sometime to him over the
desert from his own hogan built of evening light
and peace. For here also there was peace.

The days when he dwelt like a Paiute slave with Crooked Mouth seemed far away—farther than his earliest childhood here on the slope of the mesa. Though he took care never to approach the chindi hogan whose charred logs were but a few miles distant, he knew that in coming back to this place where he was born, he had, after long journeying and exile and slavery, at last come home. Here the mesa was at his back with strength. Here the gods had first known him.

Singing, he herded his sheep through the hot days. In search of grass he wandered far from the gray cliffs, and came sometimes to the trading post to water his sheep beneath that silver wheel. The trader watched him from the door of the post, and the farmer's wife sometimes spoke to him in her own tongue. Once he found the Mender of Windmills there, and talked to him in the speech of the desert.

But at evening he came back to the cliffs of the mesa and was content to be alone.

※ ※

The hot wind blew and was never still, until night laid coolness on the desert. And then with the blaze of another day the wind swept once more across the country of the People.

East toward the Lukachukai Mountains rain

hung half way to earth, like a curtain of blown gauze. But no rain fell.

On the desert the waterholes were empty, and the grass was burnt by wind and sun. The cattle and horses of the People grew lean. The flocks drifted in search of grass under a sky like a copper flame. . . .

The boy lay half asleep in the shadow and watched his sheep grazing between heights of honey colored rock. Around him was the hot dry fragrance of cedar and piñon, and through an opening in the rocks he could see the distant shaft of Agathla. The sun, noon high, blazed upon the desert between.

Suddenly the boy became alert. There in the rocks was something he had not seen. It was not honey yellow like the rocks above and the dry basin of rock beyond. Nor was it the rich green of the living trees, nor the brown of the dry spills below them. It was blue—and the boy standing now beside it saw that it was a blue bird, lying dead at the edge of the dry water hole.

But this was not the blue bird of the desert and the desert songs. This bird with the long legs was one for which he had no name. Blue, not like the sky there above the height of honey colored rock, nor like turquoise. It was more like a fragment of blue from a distant mesa at noon, or like smoke when the flame has gone.

The boy picked it up cautiously. A singer would like those feathers for his medicine bag, if they could have been plucked from the living bird. But this bird was dead, and he had no name for it.

He carried it with him when he started back again toward the cliffs of the mesa. He was carrying it when he came to the trading post.

The farmer's wife saw it in his hand as he passed, and at her call he stopped. She left the fenced yard and ran out to him, her skirt blowing in the wind. As she took the bird from him, she spoke excitedly in her own tongue. He wished the Mender of Windmills were there to interpret for him,—or even the half-breed from the trading post. Perhaps she was giving him a name for this bird with the feathers like blue smoke.

But now her voice was broken and she was crying. She wiped her eyes on her apron, but the tears still fell. Was she crying about this bird?

The sheep had gone on ahead and were drinking at the windmill trough. He must go on and start them again toward the mesa. He reached out his hand for the bird.

"No, no!" she cried sharply.

She turned toward the house and he watched her

go, carrying the bird with her. He had not brought it to her for a gift; she had run after him as he passed with the sheep. But now he watched her carry it away and was helpless.

She turned and signalled him to follow her. Slowly he went through the gate of the farmer's yard. The sheep were still drinking and moving restlessly around the windmill.

The farmer's wife came out again with a string of red and blue beads in her hand. Pointing first to the bird, she gave the beads to him.

He took them doubtfully. The bird he had wanted to show at the trading post. . . .

The beads were not turquoise and coral, he was quite sure. But they were shinier and prettier perhaps. In any case, now that she had the bird, and had given him a gift also, he did not see what he could do about it. She had turned back to the stiff bird with its ruffled feathers of smoke-blue, and she was crying again, crying with hard sobs which he did not like to watch. He put the beads around his neck and went down to his sheep at the windmill.

※ ※

Rain came at last to the desert with the smell of the first drops falling on dry dust, and then a white torrent that washed the rocks with silver and shut out the rest of the world like a blanket over a hogan door. And then came the spiced sweetness of cedar and piñon, and a breathing after the rain.

When the first green sprang up on the desert the boy found grazing land for his flock close to the mesa and seldom wandered as far as the trading post. At the nearest windmill he sometimes saw other sheep herders bringing their flocks to drink, and sometimes a horse herder driving in horses from the desert. But not until the Mender of Windmills came did he ask about the bird with the smoke-blue feathers.

"I have seen that bird," he said. "But I had no name for it, and the farmer's wife took it from me."

"I too have seen it at the farmer's house," said the Mender of Windmills. "They call it a heron. It came a long way from a place where there is much water. It came somehow to this place where there was no water; and so it died."

The boy thought for a while.

"Why did the woman cry?" he asked at last. "Why did she take the bird away from me?"

"Because she too has come from that country to the south, from the summer that follows the summer. When she saw the bird dead she wanted to go back. She cried until the farmer was angry and threw the bird away in the rocks."

The boy was silent. The Mender of Windmills worked on the pump.

"She felt as you did perhaps in the hogan of Crooked Mouth," he suggested.

"But she is not a slave," said the boy.

He turned to follow the sheep which were already moving on. For a moment he looked out across the desert, seeing it in its color and shadow. Over his shoulder he spoke again to the Mender of Windmills.

"And this land also is green after the rains."

It was time at last to gather piñon nuts on the high places of the desert; and now the boy was no longer alone.

"There is room for you in this hogan," said one of his clan. "It is not good to live so much alone. Who will tell you the stories of the great chants? Who will tell you the stories of your clan? Who will teach you the songs that wanderers have brought from the places of the gods?"

The boy at last agreed. In that hogan he lived henceforth. Often he gave them gifts of sheep or wool or the hides of goats. But when he rode with them to the trading post, he brought his own goods and received money in exchange; and there they pointed him out as the boy who owned sheep.

The boy who owned sheep had not forgotten that he was the boy at whose birth the moon fainted. Even when he was taken to a sunny hollow of the desert and beaten with soapweed and allowed that night to see that the masked gods of the rite were men, even then he did not forget.

Wandering with his sheep on the desert he felt for a little while like one of the stricken twins, who had been turned away from the hogans of the gods. But he remembered that the twins still had sung. He remembered that when they sang the talking god of dawn had looked at them with pity.

Still he listened for the four calls on the desert at break of day. Still he hoped that the god of evening would come some time to the hogan where he was. For at his birth Night Bearer had thought of him, and the moon had fainted.

The great winds blew, bringing snow at last to the country of rock and piñon. The boy, herding his sheep on the desert, saw one day a woman walking alone. And the snow was falling.

He knew by her clothing that she was not of the People. Then as he came nearer the road, he saw that she was the farmer's wife.

Far from the farmer's house and the trading post, she trudged along. But she walked as if her feet were weary with the miles. . . .

The boy's flock would be crossing the road in a moment more. He wondered that she should be so far from the trading post, this woman whose heart was sick in a strange land. Hastening the nibbling sheep on their way he tried to reach the road before she had passed. In the snow little bells sounded.

The woman did not turn her head to look at the herdboy and the slow flock coming. Even when they reached the road and were crossing it, she did not pause. Her hurrying feet pressed on through the snow.

The boy spoke to her then—a slow word of greeting. But the woman did not seem to hear. Now though the sheep were parting to let her through, she paid no heed. With eyes fixed on the snow-blurred distance, she hurried on. For a long time the boy stood watching her, until the falling snow shut her from sight.

Late in the day he came with his flock to the trading post. For a moment he went into the warm room where the men were lounging and talking with the half-breed trader.

He sat down on the mud floor and listened to them. The half-breed looked at him thoughtfully.

"Here is one they will take to school," he said.

The boy was silent, waiting.

"All day the farmer has been riding with a

school man from hogan to hogan. Only now have they come back. Twenty children of the People the school man will take back with him to the agency."

The boy was silent still.

"I stay here," he said briefly at last.

He stood at the door ready to go out, but before he left, the strangeness of the farmer's wife walking alone came to his mind. He told them that he had seen her.

"The farmer should know of this," said one. "There is something strange here."

"It is not a good thing for her to go alone over the desert," the others agreed.

The half-breed left the store to his wife, and went up the hill. When the boy started his sheep again toward the mesa he saw the farmer riding hard along the way which he and his sheep had come.

Now the boy who owned sheep herded them in remote places, and stayed away from the trading post. He knew that they would cut off his hair if they took him to school, and would forbid him to speak the language of the People.

"I stay here," he resolved again.

Through long days he herded his flock alone.

The women of his clan took his goatskins to the trader.

"The farmer has gone away," they said one day. "His house is empty and he will not come back."

An old woman nodded.

"It is a good thing," she said. "So should he have done long ago. Does not a man go to his wife's people?"

The winter winds still swept across the desert. One morning a man rode to the hogans at the foot of the mesa.

"The agent has sent word that there will be a new farmer," he said. "In the spring we can go again to the watered land and plant corn."

But through the winter they stayed on the slopes of the mesa where they could find stout cedar and piñon for their hogan fires.

The stories of the gods and of the men who had been with gods were much in the boy's mind these days. For now the lightning was asleep and the great chants were being sung on the desert. Now the old men told stories of the rites and their beginnings; and the old women told, as his grandmother had done, the stories of their clan.

Sometimes as the firelight flickered in the hogan and the great winds howled across the desert, there were tales of a nearer time. The boy watched wrinkled faces grow stern with memories of the exile.

He heard how the soldiers came even to the Canyon de Chelly, to the stronghold of the gods, and how there they cut down two thousand peach trees. He heard how they killed the flocks of the People and laid waste their cornfields. He heard how at last the land between the four sacred mountains was without defense because the people had no food.

Then those who had been living in that bitter time told of the journey to an alien land. There among strangers, hated alike by the Apaches and Comanches and Mexicans, they had known four years of sorrow. There they found no piñon and cedar for their hogan fires, but only a meager supply of roots which they dug from the ground. There they had no flocks and cornfields, but only the rations the white man gave them.

"In that time a thousand of the People died from eating the white man's food."

So said the old men, and in the hogan there was no sound but the fluttering of a flame, and the desert wind crying. The boy hugging his knees in the shadow listened breathlessly.

Then the old men told of one small band that had stayed in the desert canyons. Driven by the soldiers to the Old Age Water of the San Juan they had found it nearly dry before the desert rains. Horses and men had followed the stream bed and turned at last back again into the country from which they had come. Then the rains came, and water filled the San Juan in a raging torrent. The troops following the broad trail of the fleeing people lost it at the river. There they waited while the days slipped by, waited for the river to go down so that they could cross it in pursuit; and while they waited, the fleeing men and women, on the same side of the Old Age Water, were finding safety in the canyons. When the old men told how the troops lost the trail and turned back at last, there was laughter in the hogan, laughter from old men and old women and from the young people listening.

Someone lifted a burning twig from the fire to light his cigarette, and as it was passed around, one face after another stood out of the shadow. But the boy did not stir. He saw only the People huddled together in an alien land; and one small group free in the canyons.

The low voice went on. Now the boy saw the People coming back—back to the land guarded by the mountains where dwelt the sacred ones: the White Corn Boy and the Yellow Corn Girl, the Boy Who Carries One Grain of Corn, and the Girl

Who Carries One Turquoise, the Pollen Boy and the Grasshopper Girl. . . .

Back to the desert where they had been free, where now they would be free again. Back, fewer by a thousand than they had gone away, but men once more. . . .

The listening people in the shadow stirred. Someone put more wood on the fire, and the blaze lighted the hogan. But the boy left his sheepskin, lifted the blanket at the door and went out.

Above him were stars, flashing and then dim, and the wind swept across the desert with knives of cold. He hardly breathed as he stood there, so taut was the quietness within him, so keen was his sense of the People coming home. Suddenly he knew the desert, as at moments he had known the gods.

The boy grew, tending his flocks at the foot of the mesa through long white days, sleeping beside the fires of his clan through nights of cold starlight. Now at the great chants he was often with the men who were making prayer sticks, learning to fashion them and place them according to the will of the gods. He learned designs and colors as the singer gave his orders and the bright sands fell. Finally under the tutelage of an old man singing in the firelight, he began to learn the chanted prayers.

With eyes half closed and body tense, he sang the songs of the Wind Chant in their order. . . .

Wind and snow and the hot sun of summer noons beat upon the desert. As the boy wandered with his flock they pointed him out as the boy who owned sheep, and they said he would be a wind singer.

III

SHE was clear-eyed, and they called her the Girl Whose Eyes Are Like Rock Crystal. Like Rock Crystal—and a virgin of the People.

Windsinger saw her in the morning rite of the Entah, saw her in her white blanket leading the procession of the women and carrying in her hand the plumed staff of war. Tall and grave on his white horse, he looked upon her and desired her.

Already the time seemed long since he had helped throw a young steer and kill it for the feast. For in that hour he had ridden down from the hill into the valley of rock and sage. He had come to the hogan where the chant lifted and throbbed under the desert noon. And there he had seen her—clear-eyed and a virgin of the People.

He heard the throb of song; he returned the silent handclasp of a friend; vaguely he was aware of the circle of horses and men, the moving gleam of silver and bright velvet. But in him there was a strange stirring of life that made the morning new.

The sun blazed upon the place of song. In the distance, the wind devils marched in gray spirals across the sage. Still the horsemen gathered, and the chanting voices sounded; and nearer came the procession of women.

Windsinger's eyes were on their leader who was carrying the staff with its tuft of green and its drooping eagle's feathers. He watched her lead the way to the shelter of cedar boughs and sit down on the ground, drawing her white blanket about her.

She was young; she was clear-eyed; she was a virgin of the People.

Within the circle of seated women two sat with their hair unbound. Behind them sat two others, brushing it with bunches of dried grass. Windsinger looked at the girl with the plumed staff of war. Her hair also would be blue-black in the sun; soft and blue-black against the white blanket. . . .

He imagined the heavy coils falling, and springing dark to the stroke of the dried grass. Blue-black hair—and eyes like rock crystal. . . .

She sat there watching the women with the unbound hair. When finally the brushing stopped and the circle of women was still, she kept her eyes on the mottled sun and shadow of the earthen floor, seeming not to see the mounted men beyond the cedar shade.

Still the chanting throbbed from the hogan, rising and falling under the desert noon. He heard the neighing of a horse, and the wind's breathing.

"I would speak to you, my friend, before we leave this place."

Windsinger looked at the man at his side, and nodded.

"I will be at the shelter on the hill for food," he agreed.

Again he turned and watched the women in the silent circle, and the girl with the staff of war.

Sun and summer wind and the voices of chanting men. . . .

From the hogan came a man bearing a bowl of water to the circle of silent women. They put into it a handful of piñon spills, and it was given to the two with unbound hair. Windsinger watched them drink, and then under the shelter of a blanket bathe their legs, their arms, their breasts. He looked at the girl with the staff.

Under her white blanket, her legs would be straight and strong, her breasts firm. There was an exaltation in Windsinger that did not belong even to this place of sun and song, as he thought of her, firm of body and clear-eyed, a virgin of the People. . . .

When the bowl came to her hand, she bathed only her face, and spread the sacred mixture on her hair. Then grave and still, she sat holding the staff, while the other women bathed their faces and their hair and spread a little of the water and piñon on the hair of their children also. Slowly the bowl went around the quiet circle.

For a little while there was silence on the desert, a pause between songs. Then again the voices lifted in the hogan, lifted with new vigor in a new song. It was punctuated with sudden cries, in which the horsemen joined. Now even Windsinger looked away from the virgin leader of the women to the door of the hogan.

Once more the singers were silent; once more they renewed their song. The women with the unbound hair had been covered with white cloth and sheepskins and many blankets. The sun beat down upon the cedar shelter and upon the crowd of horsemen. Sun and dust and sage, and the rise and fall of men's voices chanting. . . .

At the door of the hogan a man appeared with a warning cry. The women hid their faces in their blankets and covered their children's eyes. From the hogan ran two men and a boy, painted black, and naked save for loincloths. They wore silver girdles about their waists and silver bracelets on their arms; and each wore a feather in his hair. Away from the crowd of horsemen in the sun, away from the circle of women in the cedar shade, ran the three naked warriors forth into the desert.

No one looked after them. There was silence in that place.

The women uncovered their faces and stood. Windsinger watched the girl with the staff of war lead them away. Straight and tall, with grave clear eyes, she walked past him. When she was gone he did not wait to watch the others go up the hill. He wheeled his white horse, and rode away across the rock and sage.

That afternoon Windsinger sat in the great cook shelter. Beside him a man was talking in slow troubled tones, paying no heed to the people coming and going.

"It is true," Windsinger told him. "I have learned the Wind Chant. But I have not led the chant alone."

"Fifteen sheep I will give you from my flock— and a cow besides, to sing the Wind Chant for my uncle."

Windsinger hesitated.

"A bracelet of silver and turquoise also," added the other.

"I will sing the Wind Chant for your uncle," agreed Windsinger.

They reached for mutton from the iron pot and ate for awhile in silence.

"What is the evil in your uncle?" asked Windsinger at last.

"He is twisted and bent and feels pain night and day. We have given sheep and silver to many singers, but they have brought no help. Now he remembers that once he built a fire of a fallen tree and ate the food cooked over it. They told him afterward that the tree fell in a whirlwind."

Windsinger's face was grave.

"It is well that I sing the Wind Chant over him. I will come—four days from this day."

"Four days," repeated the other. "It is well. My uncle will prepare."

He laid down his rib of mutton and went out. Windsinger leaned back on his sheepskin, scanning the crowd.

He could see the two women who with unbound hair had taken part in the morning ceremony. Now they sat beside one of the fires where the mutton was boiling in iron pots. He could see the men who had run forth naked into the desert. Now they were pulling on their clothes and talking with their friends. A child cried, and a young woman lifted it, still tied on its baby board, and put it to her breast. Patting great disks of dough, the old women sat beside their pots of sizzling fat. All along the sides of the dim shelter, from the end where the great quarters of raw meat were hanging, to the blankets over the door, men and women and children lay sleeping on their sheepskins.

Windsinger's eyes wandered over the crowd and came back at last to the fire. Nowhere in sight was the girl whose eyes were clear, like rock crystal. . . .

There was a song in him as he thought of her. . . . She was young, and he had sheep to bring to her mother—sheep enough even for a virgin of the People. Truly the gods had seen to it that he should have sheep enough. For his first wife he would not need to take a woman who was old, who had already had a husband and borne children to him. He looked with pity at a young man lounging on a sheepskin near him. That young man had taken for his first wife an old woman. Not until his wealth was greater could he bring a young wife to his hogan, a girl with youth in her walk and the laughter of youth in her eyes, a girl who had known no man.

But under the cliffs of the mesa a flock was grazing; and there cattle and horses were running free on the desert. The boy who owned sheep had herded them and traded them with skill. Now he was a man, and could have the girl whom he desired.

He moved restlessly and stood up. Between the sleeping men he made his way to the door, and the long valley of rock and sage was spread before him. On every small hill, in the shade of every clump of piñon, family groups were sleeping. A trader was selling cold watermelon from his wagon. A quarter of beef lay roasting on hot coals. A little girl on a burro was herding sheep in the distance, looking back over the valley with its movement of men and horses, its life where loneliness had been.

Windsinger too looked out over the sage gray distances. Somewhere among the scattered groups was the girl with the plumed staff of war. The thought of her made him forget even his joy in being asked for the first time to lead the Wind Chant.

He strode over to the white horse under a piñon tree. At his touch the firm neck arched and turned. He felt the white mane, and for a moment it was black hair, soft beneath his hand. . . .

In the valley a drum beat.

Windsinger swung into his saddle and rode slowly down the hill.

From all the camps the People were coming on horseback and on foot. Already they were gathering in a restless circle. In a shaded place the women sat waiting.

A man with a lean strong face spoke for a long time from his horse.

"There should be cornfields wherever the water runs," he said. "Look at the cornfields the Hopis have in Moenkopi Wash. Those cornfields should be ours."

The men nodded, and spoke slow words of approval as the long speech went on. Windsinger sat on his white horse and listened.

When the speech was done two men brought a dispute for settlement.

"It is true I killed his steer," said one. "But that steer had broken into my cornfield and trampled my corn. What recompense shall I have for that?"

"The steer I could have sold for much silver," insisted the other. "Your corn does not pay me for my steer."

They looked at each other angrily. First one and then the other stated his case to the assembled people.

"Let them say what price they would ask for the steer and for the corn," suggested Windsinger quietly.

"The young singer has spoken wisely," said an old man.

"The steer was a yearling," said the owner. "A yearling and worth ten dollars."

"Pay him the ten dollars; you have killed his steer," said Windsinger.

The owner of the cornfield pulled the money from the pocket of his blue trousers. Grudgingly he counted it into the hand of his antagonist.

"You are content?" asked Windsinger.

"I am content," said the owner of the steer.

Windsinger turned to the farmer.

"What of your corn? Set the price on that."

"There would have been a crop worth fifteen dollars," was the reply.

"Not so much," protested the owner of the steer.

"Fifteen dollars—no less."

The old men spoke among themselves.

"Twelve dollars I will take for my corn," said the farmer.

"Ten dollars, and no more, is fair," maintained the owner of the steer.

Windsinger nodded.

"Remember this man also has lost. You have killed his steer. Take ten dollars for your corn and be content with that."

Reluctantly the ten dollars was counted back into the hand of him who owned the cornfield.

"You have lost a corn crop and a steer," said

Windsinger. "But you have been paid ten dollars for the crop, and ten dollars for the steer. It is just."

The crowd laughed. The disputants shook hands doubtfully.

The afternoon shadows were long on the sage, when a group of men gathered and began to sing. Rising and falling in time to the beat of a gourd and a stretched skin drum, the song throbbed on the desert. Windsinger joined the growing circle, as it turned first in one direction then in the other. Moccasins and boots, cords and chaps and calico trousers circled in slow jerking steps, grayed with dust.

Still the women sat in the shadow waiting. Still the mounted men talked in little groups.

The moving circle stopped. A few men came together and sang with new earnestness. Windsinger swung again into his saddle and waited. Song throbbed around him.

At last in the long light of the setting sun he saw the girl coming, carrying the plumed staff. With slow even pace she approached the singers and the horsemen. Windsinger moved in his saddle as she came near, and for a moment her eyes rested on the tall young man on the white horse. Then she kept on and stood in front of the singers.

The song rose and fell, and the people waited.

Smiling faces were turned toward the girl who stood clear-eyed in the sunlight. . . .

She looked at the men. Then once more she looked at Windsinger on his white horse. And she did not look away.

The horses and men, the smiling women, and the distances of sage faded. Windsinger saw only the straight girl coming toward him, the steady eyes upon him. His hand tightened on the rein.

He felt the pull of her hand on his silver girdle, the tugging on his crimson blouse. Quick joy flamed within him.

He knew vaguely that he was pulling back, when every muscle in his body was tensed to go to her. He knew that he was swinging to the ground with the feigned reluctance that was expected of him. Then suddenly he knew only that he was dancing back and forth, her arm upon his. In the sunset light he was dancing with the girl who could carry the plumed stick, the girl who was young and clear-eyed. . . .

He did not see the other girls approach, nor the men who suffered themselves at last to be drawn into the dance. With the girl's hand upon his arm, he was a warrior dancing.

The light faded. The valley of sage was in shadow. Mesas and hills were silhouetted against the dim sky. And then the dance stopped, and she was gone.

Windsinger walked up the hill toward the great shelter. There the firelight played upon groups of seated people. A woman, whose bearing showed her one used to command, and a man of proud countenance moved among the people, seeing that none went hungry. As Windsinger went toward the fire, they turned to look at him.

"That is the young wind singer. The girl with the staff chose him."

The girl with the staff chose him—chose him from all the others. The knowledge of it was like the drum beating in the dance. . . . He helped himself to a mutton bone, and broke a segment of bread from the flat disks. But as he sat down to eat, he was aware of only one thing. She had chosen him.

At last he went out, and stood alone in the dark. Fires gleamed along the valley, and at the foot of the hill marching men were singing. He listened to the chant grow faint as they marched away into the distance.

Making his way slowly down the hill, he went toward the chanting men, and outside the hogan where the morning rite had been held he joined a group of singers. Another group stood opposite them. Swaying in the dark they chanted a wild antiphonal.

Men and horses came out of the night and stood black against distant fires. As the chant rose and fell, a white light spread in the east, and in the valley another chant began, throbbing to a drum far away.

Over the eastern ridge the white moon lifted. White light lay on the sage distances. At the hogan the swaying men ceased their singing, and the wild antiphonal was stilled.

Toward the other chant, still sounding in the distance, Windsinger walked over rock and sand. They had built a fire there and above the grotesque pattern of black timbers the flame rose high.

As he approached it the path for his feet was dark. But ahead of him the firelight blazed behind the moving shapes of men and horses; and in him like firelight was the knowledge that the girl with the staff of war had chosen him.

He sat down by the fire. Around him were sleeping figures, their feet to the flames. A group of men and women talked in low tones to a husband and wife who had brought a dispute for settlement. Other fires blazed nearby. And in the darkness there was song.

An old man approached him. They greeted each

other with a slow clasp of hands, and talked in the firelight.

"It is the first of many times that you will lead the Wind Chant," said the old man at last. "You are a man, and have learned well."

Windsinger was silent at this praise.

"It is my first chant and I do not forget that you have taught me," he said at last. "Fifteen sheep, a cow, and a bracelet they have offered me. I give you all these."

Two men piled more logs on the fire. The song beat with new intensity. Into the firelight the girl with the staff was coming.

Windsinger stood motionless, forgetful of the old man at his side, forgetful of the moving crowd. She had chosen him. She was coming.

The crowd moved back, leaving a cleared space beside the great fire. The chant and the beating drum throbbed on the desert. With slow pace the girl bearing the staff came near.

Windsinger hoped, and dared not hope. He turned to the old man, speaking casually.

"The cattle are lean beyond the Pass. There is nothing but dry grass for fodder."

But he did not hear the old man answer. The girl with the staff of war was near.

She stood in the cleared space, and again the eyes

of the crowd were on her. The young men stood
with their blankets wrapped about them, waiting.
By their mothers' sides the young girls stirred and
were quiet.

With calm face the girl in the white blanket
searched the faces in the firelight. Here was one
grave and proud against the flame, the face of
Windsinger, turned away from her. She walked
toward him, and again her hand was pulling his
blanket with an insistence that would not be de-
nied. Again there was flame within him.

Now he was dancing in the firelight, turning,
turning, with the girl at his side. There were
others dancing but he did not see them. There was
song in the night but he did not hear. Back and
forth, back and forth, with the girl who was young
and clear-eyed. . . .

The song ended, and for a moment they stood
together quietly. Then once more the drum
throbbed and the voices lifted. Once more they
were dancing under the desert night.

The crowd laughed as a white trader was drawn
into the dance. But as the night wore on, the trader
and his friends left, and only the People were moving in the dance of war.

Above them the night blue of the sky was yellowed with smoke and flame. Silver bracelets

clashed as the dancers stopped and turned, and moved on with shuffling feet.

The watching men and women moved closer to the fires. Off in the dark a startled horse plunged through the sage. . . .

Still Windsinger and the girl with the plumed staff danced side by side.

"Are you cold?" Windsinger asked in a low voice.

"No," she said quietly.

But he threw his blanket around her. And now under the same blanket they moved to the throb of the drum. He felt her body against his as they turned. In the pauses of the dance she did not take her hand from his arm.

The dark hours slipped by and he felt her leaning against him. But weary with dancing, the girl with the staff danced on. In the desert night she and Windsinger moved to the drum of war. . . .

The fire burned low. Under the cold sky the chanting voices sounded. But at last the shuffling feet were still. Windsinger, standing alone, watched the girl with the staff go with her mother into the darkness.

He strode again up the hill to the cook shelter. There too the fire had burned low. He moved carefully between sleeping people and dipped a cup of

hot coffee from the boiling cauldron. In the shadow
a woman moved, still busy with the cares of the
day.

Again he went out into the moonlight. He found
a place beside one of the fires, and lay down with
his blanket around him; his blanket, that had held
the clear-eyed one. . . .

The chant throbbed in the night with tremend-
ous volume and sudden fall. In the pauses one high
voice carried on, to the beat of the stretched-skin
drum.

Day broke, with cold pallor, and the chanting
voices stopped. Across the desert the singers rode
away.

The old man stood beside Windsinger.

"We will ride together through the Pass," he
said.

"It is good," Windsinger replied.

He stood up and wrapped his blanket again
around him. The firelight sifted through the piñon
boughs of the cook shelter, and around some of the
other fires men and women were preparing food.
The valley between the rocky hills held smoke in
its long embrace.

"With us as far as the Tsagi ride Red Sheep and
his wife and sons—his daughter also who carried
the staff."

"It is good," said Windsinger again.

They drank more coffee and swung into their saddles.

Against the dust colored edge of day mounted men were riding. Suddenly as Windsinger galloped across the valley the morning was blue around him; blue on the hills and mesa, blue on the drifting smoke, gray blue on the sage.

The sun swung above the ridge. Toward them a group of riders was coming, and one of them had a white blanket about her. Windsinger broke into song and the others answered. Singing, they came together, as friends in a desert place. And together they rode away into the Pass.

卍 卍

The four days passed, and Windsinger, gravely exultant, led his first chant. Now indeed he was a man, in the presence of gods. Toward this had he looked, unknowingly, when first he had felt the nearness of the divine ones on the desert. Toward this had he moved since he was a child, herding his sheep alone.

The song lifted to the beat of rattles and fell like a sigh into stillness. Steadily the voice of the young wind singer moved into the new song. And the gods were near him.

He took from his bag four sacred feathers and

pressed them with low cries against the feet and hands and head of the sick old man. The fire sank low. In the shadow the beat of rattles and the throbbing song went on. Darkness and song in the hogan—and the presence of the gods.

Suddenly, though he knew his thoughts must not wander, the young wind singer remembered the girl whose eyes were like rock crystal. For a moment the singing men were singing for a dance of war, and the girl with the staff was beside him. Then once more he was chanting for an old sick man. . . .

Song after song in their order he lifted, for the man who had used as fuel the branches of a wind-felled tree. Song after song, until body and mind had lost all memory and desire. In that hogan he was a priest of the wind rite, chanting the songs of the gods.

Riding back again to the cliffs of the mesa, the young wind singer thought once more of the girl whose eyes were clear, like rock crystal. This time he did not put the memory of her away. So vivid was it that for a moment she seemed to be riding with him once more through a blue morning. He felt an exaltation in the thought of her as keen as the exaltation of the chant. The same sharp sense of life came to him, the same clarity and tense quiet.

"Like the Rock Crystal Girl, whom the gods placed in the mountain to the white east," he thought. "Like her who gave men minds. . . ."

At the time of the summer rains he went to claim her. All night lightning had shot over the mesa, and as he set forth he could see distant showers hanging in torn shreds between near sunlight and far. The wind in his face was sweet with the fragrance of the desert waking to the rain. And he sang because it was the morning of his marriage day.

He started at a gallop, singing in time to the thudding feet of his horse. When at last he stopped and waited for the rest of the bright cavalcade, there was still song within him.

The others overtook him, and laughed at his haste. But he scarcely noticed these men and women of his clan, nor the old wind chanter who rode by his side. It was enough that the girl whose eyes were like rock crystal was waiting for him in the canyon, enough that he was going to her.

He had sent fifteen sheep and two cows to her mother, and now he led four horses and carried a string of fine turquoise. Rich gifts were these— but he sought a girl who was young, and a virgin of the People.

Away from the cliffs of the mesa they rode, out

into the lonely places of the desert. They came at last to the trading post where the half-breed trader stood in the doorway and watched them pass by.

"Listen," said the old man.

They drew rein and were quiet. In the silence sounded the roaring of the wash, bank high.

"It has been raining in the Tsagi. There too the water will be running."

Windsinger started on.

"If the wash has not gone down when we reach the Tsagi," he said quietly, "we will still go through."

"He fears another man will take her," laughed one.

"Or perhaps he fears her mother will ask more sheep for each day that he delays."

"He is young," said the old man, "and it is his marriage day."

They rode away from the wide light of the desert, and the cliffs of the Pass closed in. Now clouds covered the sun and the rain was cold and sweet upon them. They urged their horses on against the wind and rain until they came to the mouth of the Tsagi Canyon.

"We wait here," decided the old chanter. "Even a young man should see that we cannot cross."

They looked at the roaring brown torrent.

"We wait," conceded Windsinger.

The rain lashed the red cliffs with running silver. Even when the rain passed, and the thunder rumbled afar off, the water ran bank high in the wash. They built a fire then, and crowded close to dry their dripping clothes. Around them was the keen breath of piñon and cedar, and above them broken clouds hurried across the sky.

"Perhaps we ride no farther today," said the old man.

"We ride to the hogan of Red Sheep," insisted Windsinger.

Noon was long past when at last they agreed that it would be possible to ford the wash. Windsinger was first to plunge in. The water swirled as his horse felt for firm footing. Behind him the others were spurring on their mounts. Finally Windsinger felt his horse pull free of quicksand and lumber up the bank.

"We ride to the hogan of Red Sheep," he cried triumphantly to the others.

Through the afternoon they followed the trail as it crossed and recrossed the wash. Water and quicksand did not hold them back. When they reached a stretch of sheep-cropped turf they broke into a canter. Grass grew in that canyon between the red cliffs, and tall spruce, dark against the heights of rock. Wild roses bloomed there, and the fragrance of rain stayed with them as they rode.

At a turn in the canyon they saw other riders ahead. A moment later the sons of Red Sheep came galloping to meet them.

"Our sister waits for you," they said to Windsinger. "Already there is meat on the fire and a feast is prepared for your welcome."

With laughter and talk they rode forward again, until they came at last to the hogan of Red Sheep. Singing they came, to show that they were friends. As they dismounted, Windsinger glanced quickly about, seeking the face of his bride. For a moment they looked at each other, and he knew quick ecstasy. Soon, soon, would be their marriage.

Late sunlight slanted against the cliffs above them as they sat by the fire eating the roasted meat. Late sunlight, then rain again with the dusk. As night closed in, the falling rain was a presence in the dark.

The mother of the bride moved at last to prepare the marriage meal. She burned a handful of cedar twigs to ashes, and then with a bundle of dried grasses dipped in water she moistened the ashes and stirred them to a paste.

"Give me the corn meal now," she commanded quietly.

An old woman brought her a sheepskin bag. Handful by handful she added the corn meal to the mixture of ashes and water. Stirring slowly with a bunch of slender sticks, she waited for it to cook over the fire.

"It is ready," she said at last.

They brought her a shallow basket, and she poured the porridge into it. Then all together they went out from the hogan.

The rain was still falling, and lightning flashed on their path as they went to the marriage chao. New built of cedar and piñon boughs, it stood wet and fragrant in the rain. A fire flickered through the woven darkness of its walls as they came near.

At last Windsinger was seated on the ground, and the girl with the eyes like rock crystal was opposite him. Between them was the basket of cooked meal. They dipped their hands into it, and ate.

The fire burned low, and in the darkness an old man prayed. White lightning shone for a moment outside.

Now another low voice sounded. Windsinger and his young wife listened while the old man bending toward them gave them wise and kindly counsel for their married life.

They could hear the breathing of the people

crowded in the chao. The sharp tang of smoke mingled with the piñon and cedar, sweet with rain. . . .

Another prayed in the quiet night. Windsinger watched the dim firelight play on the face of the girl whom he had chosen. Voices, low with prayer, sounded in their marriage chao. At last the people went away, and left them there.

II. THE BLUE WIND

It was noon, and from the south a blue wind moved upon the desert.

I

THEY built their hogan at the foot of a high red cliff; and dark against the cliff a tall spruce stood with shade and fragrance for their days.

Peace was there, like the peace Windsinger had known at the foot of the mesa, when as a boy he had come home again. Peace more profound, for now the Clear-eyed One was with him to sing the prayer at the lighting of their fire.

Sometimes they would see her brothers riding down the canyon. Sometimes, while Windsinger stayed away from the hogan, her mother would come. But nearly always they were alone. Dwelling so, Windsinger was content.

"I wish never to go away from this canyon," he said to the Clear-eyed One. "For here is happiness such as men elsewhere do not know."

They came to him at last, asking him to sing. For a moment his desire was to refuse, to say to them,

"I cannot go, for there are many things to see to here—the sheep and the goats and the horses keep me."

Or more simply to say what was in his heart—

"Do not ask me to go away from my wife. For day and night I desire nothing else than to be with her."

But though he would have spoken so, he heard himself saying,

"I will come when four days have passed."

Then he knew that, even for the Clear-eyed One, he could not stay when he was asked to lead the Wind Chant. The discovery troubled him. He tried to speak of it to her.

"I see no one but you. I hear no one but you. I desire nothing so much as to stay here with you. Yet I see now that when they come for me to sing I must go. My life has been built for that. Can you understand me when I speak this way?"

The Clear-eyed One looked at him gravely.

"I understand that the gods have given you songs to sing," she said.

So when the fourth day came he rode away with happiness in his heart, knowing that his wife with a strange sweet wisdom understood that his going was not of his own choice, but that the gods had sent him.

He led the chant then with singleness of thought. As the shadows moved in the firelit hogan, he sang like one who was giving for the first time to the

People these songs of the divine ones. There was dignity in his bearing, though he was young and many in that place were old. There was humility, as was fitting in one who prayed to the gods.

When at last the rite was finished, and from the hogan of song he rode away, his thoughts came back to the Clear-eyed One from a long distance. But with the thought was a surging gladness. Before this time men and women of his own clan had welcomed him. Now a woman of another clan, who was yet nearer to him than they, would be waiting for him to come to her. The girl whose eyes were like rock crystal was waiting in the canyon; and once more the thought that he was a priest of the wind rite was lost in the thought that he was going to her.

Always he came back to her with this gladness. Between the journeys which he made they lived in happiness there in the canyon. Their sheep were many, for Windsinger's flock had been added to those which the mother of the Clear-eyed One had given her; and now when daylight cut the canyon's shadow, the Clear-eyed One moved among the sheep and rode off with them down the canyon.

Windsinger watched her go, riding her horse through the morning sunlight. Truly this girl whom he had chosen was one who would guard their possessions well, one who with skill would tend the flock which he had brought her.

Her fingers were never still. In the hot noons while the sheep rested beneath the shade of the spruce and aspens, or in the early evening when daylight lingered, she would be carding wool, or spinning, or weaving a bright blanket on her loom.

Windsinger also was busy with planted fields. And as the months slipped by and winter came, the messengers came more often to the canyon seeking the young singer.

"Come to us, for my uncle is sick."

"Come, and sing the Wind Chant for my wife."

His fees brought them new wealth, for he brought home more sheep, and sometimes silver and turquoise. They had cattle now roaming the desert; and men said,

"The young Windsinger has much wealth. Even when he was a child he owned sheep."

But Windsinger said to the Clear-eyed One,

"It is your labor which makes us prosper. Neither sheep nor cattle nor silver come much to my mind now that you care for them. I am a singer. It is enough."

The Clear-eyed One agreed.

"It is best that a woman manage all these things,"

she said. "It has been so always. Do not the women of the People own the flocks, and give wealth to their children?"

So Windsinger left all this to her and sang in many hogans where they asked his song of healing. He even went to old men who knew the songs of other chants.

"Teach me these also," he begged.

And because they knew him, and knew that since childhood his heart had been filled with the songs and stories of the gods, they taught him gladly.

"The young men are forgetting to learn these things," they said. "They are cutting their hair short, and not walking the path of song. But here is one whose youth leads him not away. He seeks to know the holy things."

And Windsinger began then to learn other chants, and other sand paintings.

At last there was song in his own hogan; and when the singing was over, they laid in his arms a son.

Then Windsinger in the slow desert speech said to the Clear-eyed One,

"I thought I knew what joy was. But now I know for the first time. There is pollen on my path—peace that you have given me. I have a wife. I have a son."

When the Clear-eyed One again herded sheep in the canyon and on the desert, she carried the child on her back. Laced in his baby board, and folded close in his mother's blanket, he looked out with grave eyes on the sunlit world. When he grew fretful, the Clear-eyed One, still seated on her horse, would pull up her velvet blouse and put him to her breast.

Windsinger, riding home from a chant, overtook her one day, driving the sheep and goats back into the canyon. She had the child with her. And she rode as straight and her eyes were as clear as when he had seen her first at the dance of war, a virgin of the People.

"It is good that this woman is the mother of my son," he thought. But because he had chanted prayers all day and all night long, their rhythm still beat in his heart, and he thought also,

"I give my thanks to the gods for this woman. For she is a woman such as the gods might desire. She is a woman who might bear sons to Hastseyalti, as have women of the People in old time. She is a woman fit for the Bearer of Day."

Thinking these things, he wrenched his thought with difficulty to what she was saying.

"I have taken goatskins and sold them to the trader. For my wool also he gave me money."

"It is not well to think altogether of selling and of making our goods increase," he said.

Thinking of Hastseyalti, the talking god of dawn and Hastsehogan, god of evening, and all the other dwellers in those houses made of dark cloud and crystal and rainbow, he rode on beside her.

Then the Clear-eyed One was silent, and silently when they reached the hogan she prepared the food for their evening meal.

"The gods also have desired turquoise and silver and broidered hides," she said, as they ate.

But Windsinger had forgotten the reproof that troubled her.

❧ ❧

The People had faith in the young wind singer and carried word of him to distant places. Soon his journeys took him far from the canyon and the Clear-eyed One.

He went even as far as the monastery where the missionaries lived, and went in one day to see the lighted altar. He watched the candles blaze, but after a little while went out. On the mountains of his land the Slayer of the Alien Gods strode with power; and in the canyons lived Hastseyalti who pitied all the men of the earth. The desert gods were his gods, and in their honor no candles burned, but the bright sands fell, and men sang old songs of valor.

But after this a white man came one night to the lodge of song where Windsinger was. Some there knew him and greeted him.

"This man, like those at the monastery, preaches the white man's god," they told Windsinger.

And Windsinger said,

"Then let him also pray in this place."

So the white man prayed in the firelit hogan. Then once more the songs of the desert gods sounded.

Windsinger found the Mender of Windmills weary and sick.

"Go no farther today," he urged, "but come to my hogan."

The Mender of Windmills left his wagon and tools at the mouth of the canyon, and rode with Windsinger to his hogan. There the Clear-eyed One gave him food, and he lay on soft sheepskins and slept the night through.

In the morning he could not go on. Touching him, Windsinger knew that fever was burning him and that he was ill.

"Stay here a little longer," he said. "For here

you are with friends. It is not good to ride in the snow and cold when you are sick."

So the Mender of Windmills stayed with them. The Clear-eyed One brought him food, and Windsinger watched beside him.

"I know the songs which will heal you," said Windsinger at last. "I will sing and you will be well."

He sent word forth from the canyon that he would sing for the Mender of Windmills; and because there were many who called the Mender of Windmills their friend, the hogan was filled with those who would help with his healing.

They made the prayer sticks in their order, and placed them as the gods had commanded. On the prayer sticks they sprinkled corn meal and threw meal also up toward the smokehole so that it fell back slowly across the slanting shaft of light. They made a sand painting, and placed the Mender of Windmills upon it while they sang for him; and Windsinger took feathers from his medicine bag and pressed them with low cries against the Mender of Windmills. They threw at last the coals of the fire out through the roof, and erased the sand painting until only a few spots of blurred color showed on the buff sand floor. When dark came, they sang again; and Windsinger, leading the songs, knew that his friend would have healing from the gods, and would go on his way with strength.

The next day the Mender of Windmills slept, and toward nightfall Windsinger came to him.

"Soon you will be well again. Even now you are better."

"Yes, I am better," said the Mender of Windmills. "Perhaps it is because of your songs."

In a few days he was able to go away and follow again the road between the windmills.

Then people said of Windsinger,

"Truly this man's singing has great power; for he brought healing even to the Mender of Windmills who is not of the People and does not know the holy way of song."

Again he took long journeys to sing for those who were sick, while the Clear-eyed One stayed in the canyon with the child, riding forth with the sheep in the morning, and in the evening bringing them home again.

Sometimes she took wool or hides to the trading post; and sometimes she sold there the blankets that she had been weaving. But when Windsinger came home again, he never asked her of these things, and she did not speak of them.

However, when spring came she went to her brothers and said,

"We should have corn fields here, for there is water enough. If my husband is away and needs help sometimes, will you share in the work, if part of the crop goes to you?"

They promised her their help, and when Windsinger came home she spoke to him of it.

"We should raise corn and pumpkins and watermelons," she said.

"I am much away; and I must sing often in distant places. When shall I plant fields and tend them?"

"When you are away, my brothers will give you help in return for a share of the crops. I have asked them," said the Clear-eyed One.

Windsinger looked into the fire with a troubled countenance.

"If they would work in planted fields, let them plant their own," he said at last. "We need no help. Have we not wealth enough in our flocks?"

So that summer they planted no corn nor pumpkins nor watermelons. But the Clear-eyed One herded sheep on the desert, and Windsinger chanted the songs of the gods.

The hot winds blew day after day and with the evening died. Then with another noon blue wind moved again upon the desert.

The hot winds blew and dark rain hung in

light afar off. Then at length the rain came, and there was new life where it fell.

It was at the time of the rain that song sounded once more in the canyon. And once more the Clear-eyed One bore Windsinger a son.

✹ ✹

Now Windsinger was ready to sing the new chants which he had learned; and he was called more often to distant places to lead his rites of healing. As he sang, a new thought was taking form—new and yet so strangely a part of him that it seemed to him that even as a boy he had seen this thing which was to be.

He spoke to the Clear-eyed One concerning it; for had she not understood that the gods had given him songs to sing?

"They have given me these songs," he said. "But these songs have been sung by men before. It may be that there are songs which have never yet been sung, sand paintings that have never yet been learned. The gods know these things and would teach them to men. Perhaps they would teach them to me."

His wife thought for a long time before she spoke.

"How would you find the gods?" she asked him.

"They have come to men before, and long ago

I hoped that Hastseyalti would come walking on the desert in the cool dawn; perhaps yet he will come. And in old times men have gone to the dwelling places of the gods; perhaps I may go."

The Clear-eyed One looked at the sheep huddled in the shade, looked at her elder son playing among them, and her younger son laced on his board.

"There is enough to do about our own hogan without going to the houses of the gods," she said. "It is not well to dream of such things."

"It has ever been the dreamers who have gone to the houses of the gods," said Windsinger.

After that he rode with a new light upon his face. As he had listened when he was a boy, so now he listened again for the call of Hastseyalti in the dawn, and the shuffling of the moccasined feet of the divine ones.

But the Clear-eyed One was busy with her flocks and with the children. When it came time again for the planting of fields she went to her brothers.

"Though my husband goes often on long journeys and more and more gives his time to singing, yet we would raise corn," she said to them. "Come and work in our fields, and take the part of the crop which is just."

When Windsinger came home again he found his wife's brothers working.

"Why do they plant their corn here?" he asked his wife.

"These are our fields," she said. "They will tend them and take what part of the crop is fair."

Windsinger was troubled.

"We spoke once of this," he recalled.

"Since then we have had another son," said the Clear-eyed One.

Then Windsinger looked at the boy playing among the sheep.

"He is a child, and scarcely able to walk. You think early of wealth for him."

"It is well to think of him," she said. "It is well for my brothers to help this child of their clan."

Windsinger protested no more.

"Let this thing be, since you wish it," he said. "You see clearly, and I have other matters to think about."

So in the canyon the brothers of the Clear-eyed One raised corn and pumpkins and watermelon. The Clear-eyed One tended her flock. And Windsinger brought home sheep and goats and silver and turquoise as the price of his chanting.

He was happy; for prosperity was with him, and peace. His sons were strong, and would grow soon to an age when they could herd sheep. His wife was still young and desirable. In his happiness he felt that the gods were near. But of the songs they might teach him he spoke no more to the Clear-eyed One. She was a woman and her mind was busy with her children and her flocks. How could she understand the heart of a singer?

※ ※

A white man came to the canyon seeking the houses of the Old People. He came with an interpreter to Windsinger.

"You live in this canyon," he said, "and know where these houses are. I will pay you to take me to them, and to help me while I dig in them."

But though he offered him money, Windsinger would not go.

"They are the houses of the Old People," he said. "I will not go to dig there."

When the man had gone away, Windsinger said to the Clear-eyed One,

"Did he think I would go with him to the houses of the Old People? There, it is said, the gods lived once."

"You said you wanted to go to the dwellings of the gods," said the Clear-eyed One.

When the white man began his work in the cliff ruins, he came again to their hogan; and the Clear-eyed One sold him a sheep, and promised him fresh meat when he wished it.

When Windsinger came home, she said to him,

"I have sold meat to him who digs in the houses of the Old People."

"The sheep are yours," he replied briefly. "Do with them as you will."

But though the white man came often to their hogan, Windsinger did not go to the place where he was digging.

"It is not so that I go to seek the gods in their dwelling places," he said.

※ ※

Still he sang, and still he dreamed of new songs that the gods would teach him. At last he thought of a new thing. He went to the Clear-eyed One with it, because he felt that of this she would approve.

"Our oldest son is growing. Soon it will be time for his initiation into your clan. Soon I can begin to teach him the songs of the Wind Chant. Then when I learn new songs from the gods, I can give them to him first of all; for already his feet will be set in the way of song."

"You still think of going to the gods?" asked the Clear-eyed One quietly.

"The gods will fling out a path of light for my

feet. On sunbeam and lightning I shall go to their dwelling places."

He spoke with certainty. The Clear-eyed One was silent.

"Few have gone to the hogans of the gods," she said at last.

"That is true. But the gods have already thought of me. They thought of me at my birth, when the moon fainted. They will come for me."

The Clear-eyed One carded wool with increased vigor. At last Windsinger spoke sadly.

"You do not answer me as you did when we were first married," he said. "Then you said yourself that the gods had given me songs to sing. Now, when I think of new songs and would give them to our son, you are silent."

"Then you thought not only of chanting but of your wife also," said the Clear-eyed One.

"Still I think of my wife," Windsinger replied.

"To give you food; to give you sons," said the Clear-eyed One.

Windsinger looked at her helplessly.

"You would have me forget the gods?" he asked. "You would have me forsake the way of song that I have followed? Then truly you would have half a man for your husband. You are a woman such as the gods might have chosen. Instead, they gave you to me. And they have chosen me to sing their songs, chosen your son to pass them on."

The Clear-eyed One threw her carder down on the heap of wool.

"I have married a dreamer," she said. "But my son shall be more than a dreamer of dreams."

"You would not have a new chant to be handed down in your clan, to be passed on to your son and your son's son?"

"I would have him plant corn when it is time. I would have him think sometimes of his family, of his mother, of his wife. Give him no songs."

She went out of the hogan, and left Windsinger with bowed head. In him was a new loneliness.

ꙮ ꙮ

The children grew and at last the older son came to an age when he could herd sheep alone. Then the Clear-eyed One sat longer before her loom, weaving bright blankets as long as daylight lasted.

"For you, my son, can take the flock out into the Pass, and bring it back safely when evening comes."

The boy learned pride in his sheep and took care that none should stray. The Clear-eyed One was content.

"See," she said to Windsinger. "This son of ours can be trusted. He is like a man."

Their youngest son grew also, until he too was able to go forth with the sheep. Sometimes the Clear-eyed One, riding from the canyon to the trading post at the end of the Pass, took the two boys with her.

"It is well that you should learn to trade," she said. "When you are men you must do this often."

So they learned to count money at the trading post, and to know the value of goatskins and sheepskins, of wool and woven blankets.

At last she sent her older son alone.

"Take these goatskins to the trader. Watch him when he weighs them. See that he gives you enough for them."

The boy took pride in bringing back to the Clear-eyed One silver coins and food, and rejoiced at her praise when she said,

"Now you can make these trips to the trading post and trade as well as I."

One day, however, the boys stayed in the canyon.

"Today your uncle is sick," said the Clear-eyed One, "Your father will lead a chant for him."

She went to her brother's hogan and prepared food for those who came. And many rode up the canyon trail to sing.

Windsinger's sons watched him as he gave his quiet orders to the men who made the prayer sticks, and they saw the obedience which was given him unquestioningly.

When the bright sands fell in sure design, it was their father who guided the work. When a line was false, it was he who covered it with the buff sand of the background and commanded that it be done over.

"The singer is our father," they told the visiting children.

When the sand painting was finished and the women were permitted to enter the hogan, even the Clear-eyed One sat reverently silent.

Windsinger placed the prayer sticks in the hands of his brother-in-law and prayed. Slowly at first the phrases came, with the sick man repeating them after the singer; then faster until their voices sounded together in that place of song and prayer. While they prayed, no man stirred or spoke.

Afterward there was chanting, and as the songs sounded steadily Windsinger painted the body of his brother-in-law with lines of banded color—blue and white and black and yellow. With swift movements he tied turquoise and shell into the unbound hair of the sick man. Always in the pauses of the chant, his voice carried on.

"It is our father who sings," whispered Windsinger's sons.

Windsinger took a hot coal from the fire and placed it between the feet of the sick man. In silence he quenched it with water and threw it upward through the smokehole.

The chanting sounded again, and as the afternoon light slanted through the smokehole, Windsinger rubbed out the sand painting. In a moment there was nothing left of the pictured sun and moon, the breath of summer and winter, and the stars in the black night sky; nothing left of the pictured tobacco, and the corn and beans and pumpkins; nothing of all that color and design, save blurred spots on the floor.

But that night in the firelit hogan song still sounded. The sons of the singer watched him. Was this indeed their father, who seemed not to see them, but sang with a tense look of reverence in the presence of the gods? They were very quiet as the fire burned low and in the shadow the chanting voices swung into song after song. They slept at last, side by side on the sheepskins, hearing in their last waking moments the voice of their father, priest of the rite, singer of songs.

A few days later Windsinger and the Clear-eyed One sat at dusk watching the sheep come home. They could hear their older son singing.

Windsinger leaned forward, listening.

"That song our son sings is a song from the chant he heard. That is a song from the Path of the Spirits."

The Clear-eyed One said nothing; but Windsinger's face was alight with joy.

"Come, my son," he called.

When the boy came near he said to him,

"Perhaps you would like to know other songs of that chant. I will teach you those songs, and the sand paintings also."

The boy hesitated.

"Or, if you would like it better, I will teach you the songs of the Wind Chant. Speak, my son, what is in your thought."

The boy looked at his father gravely.

"Teach me the Wind Chant," he said, "so that I too may be a wind singer."

Then Windsinger was no longer lonely. For his elder son walked with him on the path of song.

※ ※

"I go on a long journey to sing for one who is sick," Windsinger said to the boy at last. "On this journey you too may come."

Then with wonder and delight the boy saw distant places of the desert.

They passed a horse one day, lying dead upon the ground.

"That horse was struck by lightning," said Windsinger. "When a man dies so, no one comes near; for the gods have killed him."

Once a whirlwind came toward them. When Windsinger saw the moving spiral of sand he began to sing; and when the whirlwind had swerved away, he said to his son,

"A spirit passes there."

So the boy learned the mysteries of lightning and of wind. But chiefly he learned the songs of the Wind Chant in their order. And now he boasted to the other children,

"The singer is my father. I too am learning the chant and will be a wind singer."

He brought back to the canyon tales of his journey,—the horse struck by lightning, the whirlwind which, but for his father's song, might have reached them as they rode upon the desert, the children who envied him because so young he was learning the songs of the Wind Chant.

The Clear-eyed One listened and did not reprove him. But when her younger son came home at dusk with the sheep, she turned to Windsinger and said,

"See, I have still a son."

So their wealth grew as under the wind-bright skies of summer and the gray storms of winter the

Clear-eyed One carded and spun and wove and tended the flock, and Windsinger brought home the rewards of his chanting.

Then came one to the canyon who wore clothing that was ragged and without silver. He said to Windsinger,

"I have no silver nor turquoise, and all my flock has gone to singers. But my mother is still sick. I have heard that your singing has power. What can I give you to sing for her?"

Windsinger considered the matter in silence.

"The gods have commanded that a price be paid for healing," he said at last. "Because the twins brought no gifts they were turned away from the houses of the gods, still blind, still lame."

The supplicant turned sadly away. The Clear-eyed One looked at her husband with surprise.

"But one god pitied them as they went away," continued Windsinger. "Hastseyalti, the Talking God of Dawn, will not condemn me if I go to your mother. For the price—"

Once more he was silent while he considered.

"You have bread of piñon nuts?" he asked.

"Good bread," replied the ragged one.

"Then give me a small loaf of bread when I come. That will be enough."

The ragged one went away rejoicing.

"Like Hastseyalti you have pity for men," he said.

"Pity that will make you poor also," added the Clear-eyed One when their visitor was gone.

But Windsinger reproved her.

"Always you think of wealth, my wife, when already we have enough. Always you think harshly of me when I listen to the gods."

"When the gods speak, I will not reprove you," said the Clear-eyed One.

"The gods will speak," replied Windsinger. "But even when they are silent I know in such matters the way they would have me take."

So Windsinger sang for the mother of the man who had come to him in poverty, and took in payment only a loaf made from piñon nuts.

After that another said to him,

"I have no wealth, save these buttons made of silver. But if you will sing for my uncle I will give you these. I have heard men say that for so little you will come to those who need you."

"It is enough," said Windsinger.

Again he sang, and brought home to the canyon only four silver buttons as his reward.

Then his fame went forth over the desert, and from the valley of great rocks to the hogans beyond the mesa men said of him,

"Here is a singer who will go even to the poor, and sing for them as if they were rich. He will sing the chant that is needed though you pay him only a loaf of bread or a few silver buttons."

Because he came to those who had neither flocks nor silver nor turquoise, they loved him and trusted him. As he rode the desert trails they came to him asking not only song, but judgment in their disputes and counsel in their troubles.

Yet when he rode back to the canyon, the Clear-eyed One said to him,

"Few sheep do you add now to our flocks, and of silver and turquoise I have seen nothing for many days."

"Of sheep and silver we have plenty," he told her again. "But out on the desert there has been little rain and the flocks of the People are lean. Where will they find wealth to give away, even for chants of healing?"

Seldom now did he speak to her of the gods, nor of the pity which Hastseyalti had for men. To his elder son he spoke of these things. But of what he felt most deeply he said nothing.

"For the Clear-eyed One looks at the world like a woman; and my son is still too young to understand my heart. I walk alone on the trail of song."

II

SO it happened that he told no one of a plan which he was shaping. But as he rode the desert trails it was more and more in his own mind, born of his dream of going to the gods, built on his dream of song.

"I will seek the holy ones in the houses of the Old People," he decided. "Perhaps there they will speak to me."

Under the hot winds of summer this thought was like a cool stream of running water.

"Not with a white man who goes there to dig," he thought scornfully. "Not so will I go. But alone, with songs."

As the plan grew he knew a strange happiness, thinking that the years of waiting would be ended and the tense desire of his heart would be eased. On that easing he scarcely dared to think.

Would it be the Black God of Fire whom he would see, sitting with his back to the flames; or Water Sprinkler, carrying his jar of all waters from lakes and rivers and rain? Even Hastsehogan, god of the yellow evening, or Hastseyalti, white with dawn, might come to him and lead him to the sacred hogans—hogans built of corn pollen with doorways of daylight, hogans built of black water with doorways of wind.

But he would wait no longer for them to visit the fire of his own hogan. He would go instead to the place where once they had dwelt, where others had found them. He would set forth on a lonely quest; and at its end he would find the gods.

At last he set the day for his journey, and when he was asked to sing, he refused, saying,

"I go elsewhere that day to sing."

"Then come to us afterward," was the reply.

Windsinger gave no promise.

"I will send a messenger to you," he said. "He will tell you when I will come."

For he remembered that others had been thought dead by their families, so long had they dwelt in the hogans of the gods, and when they returned they had been welcomed as people half forgotten. He would prepare for a journey of many days.

To the Clear-eyed One he only said,

"I go away to sing."

Time enough to tell her that he was going to the sacred hogans, seeking new songs from the gods. When he came home again, he would tell her that.

She gave him food for his journey and questioned him no more when he bathed ceremonially in the sweat hogan and washed his hair in suds of the yucca root. Only when he put on his silver girdle and his silver bracelets, and put a necklace of turquoise around his neck, did she speak again.

"You wear much silver and turquoise on this journey."

"There is much silver and turquoise where I go," he said.

"See that you ask a price for your singing," replied the Clear-eyed One.

Should he tell her now that he arrayed himself for a journey to the gods? He decided once more against it. Too often had she scorned him. He would not start with her mockery in his ears. When he came home again and told her that his dream of going to the gods was more than a dream, there would be no room for mockery. The Clear-eyed One herself would rejoice with him, and his son would learn his songs.

He rode down the canyon. But instead of going out into the Pass he turned aside between high red cliffs. High on the canyon wall he saw one ruin, hardly visible against the warm red sandstone, with black empty windows looking down upon him. But that ruin he passed by.

Along the trail of rock and sand he rode. He crossed and recrossed the wash. He climbed steep banks and trotted swiftly along stretches of green grass. The music of a waterfall was in his ears and then the rich voice of the wind moving in the canyon. At last he looked up, and against the red of cliff and crumbling walls he saw black windows. Here was the ruin he sought. Here in a high arched cave was the dwelling of the Old People.

The sun was low, and soon darkness would fill the canyon. But Windsinger climbed on foot up the steep side of the cliff, past the trickling spring, until the great arch of the cave was above him.

Below him was a moving mass of green aspen and oak, and the deep toned wind sounded there. But in the cave was silence.

Windsinger stepped out on the narrow trail that forgotten feet had worn on rock, and in a moment he stood on a roof that forgotten hands had built. He had reached the houses of the Old People, houses where the gods had lived.

Hushed in spirit he waited for the gods to speak. The silence of old years was there. . . .

Suddenly he turned and stared at the back of the cave. Horses' hoofs had sounded on that face of rock. Again he heard them, but he saw no horse. Would the gods come riding? He stood there trembling, ready for flight. But he did not flee.

Once more the horses' hoofs sounded. The fourth

time he should see them; for after the fourth call the gods always came. If, instead of striding on moccasined feet as in the old days, the gods came riding, even now they should be at hand. Even now they should come between him and the face of rock. Perhaps the rock itself would open, and he would look into a land of green trees and distant showers. Such lands had men seen who had seen the gods.

For the fourth time the horses' hoofs sounded. Below him the wind moved and filled the great height of the cave like a breathing presence. Windsinger was still, awaiting the gods.

He heard at last a horse walking slowly away, walking not on rock but on gravel, not in the cave but on the canyon floor. And he knew that he had heard his own horse far below.

Suddenly relaxed, he moved on. He climbed from roof to roof, over red sandstone and wattled sticks. Then once more he was quiet, seeking the gods.

The yellow evening lay on the red cliffs and on the green trees far below. The wind with the coming of evening died. On the silent ruin stood the man of the People who had come to the place of the Divine Ones.

As the dusk deepened, he began to sing, and the low song throbbed like the beating heart of that silent place. But there was no answer to his song.

Suddenly he felt the darkness filling the high cave, the shadow of night rising from the canyon. He turned and hurried back over the worn rock trail. Away from the cliff house, down from the high arched cave to the canyon floor he fled. For he knew that, though the gods had thought of him at his birth and the moon had fainted, he could not stay in the houses of the Old People when night came.

On the canyon floor he built a fire, and beside it he kept watch while the line of moonlight moved down the western cliff and up the eastern cliff as the moon rose and set. Beside the fire he kept watch all that night until at last to the canyon the cold dawn came.

In the dawn he climbed again to the house of the Old People, singing. Through another day he waited for the gods who had thought of him at his birth.

He climbed even into the small dark rooms, smelling their ancient odor and feeling the débris of corn and nuts beneath his feet. But even there no voice spoke to him out of the shadows. He peered through the tiny windows whose jagged edges framed bits of the opposite canyon wall, warm with sunlight. Suddenly the cramped darkness in which he stood seemed filled with menace and once more he climbed out into the day.

He thought of those others who had found the sacred dwelling places. One had been hunting when the gods spoke. He too might hunt, down in that canyon of green aspen and oak. But he had hunted many times, and the gods had not spoken. Here he would stay and wait for their voices. Here he would wait the guide to the hogans of cloud and crystal.

The deep voice of the wind sounded through the long hours. A bird's call fell into the quietness. Sometimes Windsinger chanted; sometimes he was silent. But neither in song nor in silence did the gods speak.

At last he decided upon a new thing. When darkness came he would not go down the face of the cliff to build his fire at its foot. Through the dark hours he would stay alone in that high cave of quiet ruin. In the night he would sing again, and the gods would come.

Late sunlight touched the houses on the cliff and the man who waited there. Then the sun was gone and the long canyon twilight was at hand, blue with day, yellow at last with evening. Still he waited, and did not flee when darkness fell.

In the darkness he sang again—sang and was quiet, tensely waiting for sight or sound of the holy ones. But he saw only the dark arch of the cave flung high against the stars, and across the canyon a ragged edge of moonlit cliff cutting the night sky. Shadow filled the canyon and the dark height of the cave. In the shadow he felt the gods near.

The hours passed, measured by the creeping of moonlight down the cliff. But in the westward-facing cave the moon itself was still unseen. In the darkness there was song, and there was silence. An owl hooted in the canyon. Then quietness closed in, unbroken.

Windsinger sat silent, keyed to a pitch where even song was forgotten. In him was longing, tense almost to pain. In him was a sense of coming wonder, close to ecstasy.

The moon swung above the canyon, filling it with light. Across the space of sky and down at last behind the rim of cliff it moved; and the shadow climbed the eastern cliff and filled the cave again. Still he sat, knowing the gods were near.

Then when the night was old, he saw, beyond the edge of the cave, pale light that was not moonlight, pale columns of light in the north, moving out from the edge of the cave and mounting free to the sky.

"Now the gods come!" he cried. "They come on the path of light!"

A path of light that would reach him soon, spanning the canyon and mesa, leading to hogans of cloud; a path of light, coming nearer.

In the silence song rang out exultant. And while he sang, the pale light moved.

So in old time the gods had spread for the feet of men bridges of sunbeam and rainbow. Now had the gods heard him also, this man of the People who had sought them.

Chanting he walked over the roofs, over the sloping floor of the cave. Closer he came to the base of that high arch flung against night and stars. Beyond the height of rock the pale light moved.

Light marching westward . . . soon it would be flung across the canyon. Out from the cliff he would step on light—light made hard enough to bear his weight as he marched to the hogans of the gods. . . .

While he waited, the shaft of pallor moved back again, back to the dark north wall of the cave.

Windsinger turned and ran back over the rock trail, out from the high arch of the cave, and down, down into the canyon. Rocks slipped from under his feet and hurtled down into shadow. Thickets of sage tore at him and branches of young spruce whipped his face.

Now he could look north between the heights of canyon wall. Now he could see the pale columns rising from a lake of white light. He could see red light also, dull and distant.

North along the canyon floor he ran, stumbling and breathless. The marching columns of light seemed once more to come near. Soon, soon, they would bend toward him, firm for his feet to travel to the hogans of the gods.

Under the aspen and oak he could not see. But out again on smooth ground, clear of trees and thickets, he ran. Still the white light beckoned. Still it urged him on. . . .

For this had he been born; for this had he lived. Fulfillment of all that a boy had dreamed, tending his flock on the desert. Answer to all that a man had hoped, chanting the songs of the gods.

He stood still again, singing in the canyon's shadow, singing as the far light flared. . . .

But as he sang the rose light faded and the white shafts sank. Lower and lower in the northern sky, farther from the feet of the searching man. . . .

Again he ran, across the shallow stream of running water, over rock and root and catching thorn.

"Hastseyalti! I am here, here!" he cried.

But he ran alone in the darkness, and the pale light dimmed.

The way to the sacred hogans was there in that dim north. But still it retreated, until the sky once more was made of night and stars, and the gods were gone.

Windsinger fell exhausted upon the ground. Over the rocks near by went the cool flow of water, and the wind stirred the leaves of aspen and oak.

Day came with cold light to the canyon. Then Windsinger arose. In him was a great exaltation. The gods had shown him their path of light, a pale shaft that another day would span the distance to their sacred hogans.

He did not sing as he rode down the canyon. The memory of the night's splendor was enough. Like song it throbbed within him.

At his birth the gods had thought of him; and now again their thought of him had been drawn as in sand upon the sky. The gods had shown him the path of light and he would yet walk upon it.

He spurred his horse to a gallop, hurrying along the canyon trail to the Clear-eyed One.

When he came at last to his own hogan and saw the Clear-eyed One waiting for him, he found suddenly that he wished to hold close this memory of the light-filled night, to know alone for a little while this joy to which a lonely trail had brought him.

He sat down in silence, watching the Clear-eyed

One as she worked at her loom, watching his elder son in the cornfield close at hand.

The Clear-eyed One spoke to him at last.

"You have come quickly home from the place of the chant."

"It was not so far as I thought," he said.

He delayed a little longer the moment of joyous recital. But he began to think of the gladness which the Clear-eyed One too would feel. While she prepared him food, he took new delight in the certainty that now she would not scorn him, now she would know that his dream was more than a dream.

"The velvet of your blouse is torn," she said.

Looking down, he discovered that it was true.

"I have forgotten how it was torn," he replied.

He ate the food which she brought him. The common things about him seemed to him beautiful. The loom with its half woven blanket, the sheepskins on the ground, the grinding stone near him—all these things he had seen and hardly noticed. But now it was as if the gods had touched them. The gods had shown him their path of light; over it they might come even to this place.

"You brought home silver and turquoise?" asked the Clear-eyed One.

"Neither silver nor turquoise," replied Windsinger.

The Clear-eyed One looked at him with scorn.

"You said there was much wealth in the hogan where you were going."

"That is true," replied Windsinger. "The gods have much wealth."

"We spoke then not of gods but of men," said the Clear-eyed One.

"I spoke of gods," replied Windsinger. "I set forth to find their dwelling place."

The Clear-eyed One turned to her loom.

"Long ago you spoke to me of such a search. But long ago you forgot it again. So I thought."

"It has never been far from my mind," said Windsinger. "When last I left this place, I went seeking the holy ones."

"You came home again," the Clear-eyed One remarked.

Windsinger paused before he answered, savoring the quick delight that would be in her face when he told her of the path of light. The time for telling her had come.

"I came home again," he admitted quietly. "But not before the gods had shown me the way of light stretching to their dwelling place."

He waited for her exclamation of surprise. But she was silent. The Clear-eyed One, however, heard all things quietly.

"I went to the house of the Old People," he said, "seeking there the gods. I stayed until it was dark and then built my fire below. I stayed through the next day, and when again it was dark, I did not go away. All night I stayed in the house of the Old People."

He waited again. Still the Clear-eyed One was silent.

"While I waited, I sang," he went on. "And before it was day, I saw the path of light. It was far away and I could not reach it. But I saw the light that the gods have ever stretched for the feet of those who sought them."

He stood up and lifted his arms to the sky.

"There in the northern sky the white light stretched. The gods have thought of me. Soon, soon, it will come to my very feet and I shall walk upon it."

The exaltation on his face was like the exaltation of a chant. But still the Clear-eyed One was silent.

"Speak to me, my wife. Speak, that I may hear you rejoice also."

The Clear-eyed One gazed steadily at him.

"I too saw the light in the sky," she said.

Then in Windsinger there was new joy.

"The gods have remembered us both; together we will go to the hogans of the holy ones."

"I saw the light in the sky—but I have seen it before. You too have seen it. For such light comes sometimes in the north."

The Clear-eyed One spoke quietly; but in her voice was denial of the vision.

"You do not understand, my wife," protested Windsinger. "There is light sometimes in the north —but this light was from the gods. It came in answer to my song."

He looked out at the cornfield and saw his son working.

"Come, my son," he called. "I would have you hear this thing."

When the boy answered his call and came to him from the cornfield, Windsinger told him also of the path of light.

"On that path I shall walk some day," he said again. "I shall bring back songs from the gods. You will sing the songs, my son."

"A new chant!" cried the boy.

"A new chant, and new sand paintings. These we can give to the People."

In his son's joy Windsinger found the response that lighted his own exaltation anew. Again the hogan seemed touched with beauty, fit for the coming of the divine ones. Above the canyon the clouds were veiling the sun and he felt their promise of rain to the desert. A vivid sense of cloud and cliff and swaying spruce poured in upon him, as if his sight had been blurred and was at last clear, as if after long climbing he had come out upon a high place.

"I walk with gods," he said.

The Clear-eyed One turned to him.

"When have you seen the gods?" she demanded.

The abrupt question crashed in upon the stillness of his heart. He looked at her silently.

"When have you seen the gods?" she repeated. "You who talk of learning songs from them! When have they given you a song?"

He tried to answer.

"I sing the songs they have given to the People——"

"To the People! To other men, who are long since under ground! You have learned your songs from men. What have you learned from the gods?"

He looked at her helplessly.

"When have they singled you out beyond other men," she demanded, "you who think yourself chosen by them?"

He made a swift gesture of protest.

"They have shown me their path of light, as they have to those others who learned their songs."

"A path of light that I too saw! A path of light

that all men have seen. Let them show you something more than light in the north!"

"They thought of me at my birth; for the moon fainted."

"Often has the moon fainted when a child was born, and the child was killed. Better that you had been killed, according to the old men's wisdom, than live your years seeking the gods whom men cannot find."

She turned to their son, standing silent and bewildered.

"You too he would fill with these thoughts, and make you a dreamer who were born a man."

Again she turned to Windsinger.

"Tell me, you who seek the gods! Has the moon fainted at any time save when you were born?"

"Yes," said Windsinger.

"Tell me this also. Does any story of the gods, or any wisdom of the old men, say that a child born then is chosen to go to the sacred hogans?"

"No," said Windsinger. "The stories of the great chants and the wisdom of the old men have not told me this."

"Then speak once more the truth. Have the old men or the gods said that you were chosen?"

"The gods have not spoken," said Windsinger. "But they showed me a path of light. . . ."

"I ask you another thing. Have you not seen light in the north before?"

"Yes," said Windsinger.

"Light such as you saw last night from the house of the Old People?"

"Like that—but never before sent by the gods."

The Clear-eyed One's voice went on with calm insistence.

"Speak truth once more. Did any god speak to you last night, saying that you looked upon the way to the sacred hogans? Hastseyalti perhaps? Or Hastsehogan? Or Water Sprinkler with his jar of all waters?"

"No god spoke," said Windsinger heavily.

"Then listen to me, my husband, while I also speak truth. No god has spoken to you. No song have you ever learned from the divine ones. No light have you seen, beyond what all men have seen. In no way are you different from other men of the People. Is this not truth I speak?"

Windsinger's head was bowed in despair. His exaltation was gone, leaving him in cold darkness of spirit. While the Clear-eyed One waited for his answer, the voice of their older son rang out, sharp with bewilderment and disappointment.

"Will you bring me no song from the gods?"

Windsinger heard the cry and looked up. In the

silence thunder sounded far off, and the first drops
of rain fell.

Slowly, heavily, Windsinger's answer came. It
came from the bleakness of his spirit.

"I do not know the way to the gods."

Then because of the boy's bewilderment and
pain, he spoke again.

"Perhaps even yet I shall find the way, and bring
you songs."

But in his heart he knew that he spoke to comfort the boy, and there was no comfort for himself.
Such loneliness was in him that it brought no added
pain when the Clear-eyed One turned to him in
scorn.

"You still seek the sacred hogans? You still think
yourself chosen by the gods to give new songs to
the People? I have listened to you long enough.
Since our marriage I have heard nothing save this
foolishness. Better if you had not seen me in the
dance of war. Better if you had not come to me in
the canyon. What have you been to me? A husband,
planting corn, bringing increase in horses and cattle? You bring not even silver and turquoise from
your chants. But always you go forth on the desert
singing for those who pay you only with a loaf of
bread. Always you come back with nothing but
dreams, dreams of going to the gods."

Passionately she turned from him to their son.

"Even my son you would take from me, making him a dreamer too. This child of my clan you would fill with dreams and songs. I taught him to herd sheep and to deal with traders. I taught him the ways of men. And now he thinks like you only of new songs that you will bring him from the gods.

"From the gods, though men have not found the way to their dwelling place since long ago, and you can do no more than other men! Such foolishness you have spoken through the years. Now when I show you truth, still you do not hear me. Still you speak of finding a way to the holy ones.'

Breathlessly she paused. But Windsinger spoke no word.

"Stay no longer in this hogan," said the Clear-eyed One. "Go to the people of your own clan. Seek if you will a path of lightning and sunbeam. Go! Go to the hogans of the gods!"

III. THE YELLOW WIND

From the yellow west a chill wind blew; and it was evening.

I

AS Windsinger rode away from the canyon of wild roses, he remembered the day he had come, his heart afire with the thought of the girl whose eyes were like rock crystal. Then too the rain had been falling. And now in the rain he rode away.

His wife's voice rang in his ears——

"Go! Go to the hogans of the gods."

The scorn in it was like a knife striking cold to the heart of his dream. Around him the day was gray with storm and there was no sweetness in the rain.

"Go! Go to the hogans of the gods."

To the rhythm of her voice his horse's hoofs pounded, now sharp on rock, now dull on sand. This then was the end of the hope that had been in him since as a boy he had tended his sheep below the cliffs of the mesa, since as a boy he had sought the gods on the desert. This was the day, cold and clear after a dream of the night.

He had no heart to defend the dream nor to resent the awakening. In him was only an aching acceptance of truth. With dull pain he saw his old

defiance of Crooked Mouth as a boy's boasting——
"I am not afraid; for I walk with gods."

How empty now that proud faith, which like a chanted prayer had filled his youth. In that moment he hated the boy who had listened in cold dawns for the call of the god of day, who had waited at sundown for the step of the god of night. He hated the man who had built his years on the hope of a journey over sunbeam and lightning to the dwelling places of the divine ones. The gods themselves must be laughing at him now, laughing at the man of the People who had dreamed of finding them as had men of old. Hastseyalti, god of day, Hastehogan, god of night, Water Sprinkler and the Black God of Fire, all of them laughing, laughing. . . .

Now indeed he saw clearly with the eyes of the clear-eyed woman.

"Go," she had said to him. "Go to the hogans of the gods."

But he could not go. The way to the sacred hogans was dark, and no path of light was flung out for his feet. She had known it, the clear-eyed woman. Now he too knew it. And the gods were laughing at his pride, and at his pain.

Quicksand clutched at his horse's feet as the trail crossed the wash. Water swirled around his legs be-

fore he climbed the bank. But Windsinger rode on
through the rain.

The gods were laughing. . . . He too could laugh.
Suddenly, echoing and re-echoing from the cliffs of
the canyon, his laughter sounded.

Let the gods mock him—let the People mock
him. Let the desert shake to the shout and scorn of
gods and men. He too could laugh at the man he
had been. Laugh with the gods—laugh like a god.
Up there in the cliff house of the Old People, let the
divine ones hear him, the man of the desert who had
sought them.

Bitter laughter, mad laughter, filled the canyon
and fell back from the high red cliffs.

When at last he reached the trading post, late
sunlight lay on the desert, filling with yellow light
the standing pools of rain. From the yellow west a
chill wind blew; and it was evening.

Still Windsinger rode through a gray world from
which the gods had gone. To ease the bleak loneliness of his spirit he stopped for a little while at the
trading post. But though the trader greeted him
when he opened the door, and the men on the piles
of wool moved over to give him room, he found no
word to say to them. Alone, infinitely far from
them, he sat in silence. Not here would he find

warmth for the cold numbness of his spirit. At last he went away.

Darkness had fallen when he swung again into his saddle. The chill wind carried the promise of rain once more. Over the mesa lightning shot in blades of fire.

As he rode, his horse's gait still pounded the bitter refrain,

"Go! Go to the hogans of the gods."

But now the mad pain of his broken dream had dulled. No longer did he laugh in the wide silence of the desert. Riding over sand hillocks and through pools of water, he rode in silence. For the first time in his life, he rode at night with no song upon his lips. Beside the tread of his horse there was no sound, save thunder far away.

The rain came again, cold on the gusty wind; rain plunging earthward, cold and hard. With each crack of thunder a blade of lightning cut the dark between him and the mesa. Again and again the horse turned his back to the wind and rain and blinding light. Still Windsinger urged him forward.

He would go to the mesa, whose cliffs had been staunch at his back in the years of his childhood. At the foot of the mesa he would find perhaps that peace he had known when he herded his sheep alone.

Then once more with bitter clarity he knew that the peace of those years was gone. Peace, born of the knowledge that the gods had thought of him at his birth and had destined him for a brave journey on a path of light. Peace, rhythmic with songs that he would bring back from gods to men. Peace built on a child's pride, and brief as the structure of a child's hogan built in play, false as a child's sand painting in a desert noon.

Thunder crashed above him as he rode through the storm. Lightning ripped the black night asunder with swift white blades. Windsinger, hopeless and alone, rode on.

Suddenly he was tired, spent with a weariness such as he had never known. No hard journeys across rock and sand had brought him such exhaustion of body. No days and nights of song and prayer had left him so drained of spirit. Slumped in his saddle, he knew for the first time weariness. With the gods gone, he was a child again, alone in the desert dark.

In his weariness and in his loneliness he remembered the twins who had been turned away by the gods. He remembered Hastseyalti, the talking god of dawn, who had looked at them with pity; Hastseyalti, who pitied all the men of the earth.

"He would look with pity upon me," he thought.

"He would not laugh because I sought him with song."

Then around him the rain and thunder roared. A white blade of light stabbed the dark. And horse and rider lay quiet upon the desert.

In the morning sunlight the Son of the Eagle rode from the mesa to the trading post. Riding swiftly, he came upon the still figures. The horse did not move as he approached. The man, stripped of his clothing, lay as one dead.

The Son of the Eagle rode at a gallop away from that place of death. At the trading post he swung from his saddle and called to the men within.

"Windsinger has been killed—killed by lightning from the sky."

They came out, looking at him with startled faces.

"He rode this way last night," said one.

"He was here, but he spoke to no man——"

They mounted their horses and rode away, guided by the Son of the Eagle. When they saw at a distance the still bodies of the horse and his rider, they drew rein and waited for the oldest among them to speak.

"The gods have killed him," said the old man. "Let the gods take care of him."

"So have men done always," the others agreed. "So will we do."

Turning, they rode back to the trading post, and left Windsinger to the gods.

II

ON the desert a prophet cried a warning to the People.

He lifted the blanket over the door of a lodge of song.

"Flee!" he cried. "Flee with your flocks and herds to the mountains. The great waters are rising to cover the earth."

The singers ceased and sprang to their feet to stare at the strange figure in the firelight. With his hair hanging loose, naked except for a loin cloth, he stood like a figure of doom.

"I have gone on a path of white lightning to the dwelling places of the gods," he cried. "I have learned from them of the great water. Flee! Flee to the mesas and the mountains!"

As suddenly as he had come, he was gone. They heard the pounding of hoofs grow faint and fade in the distance.

"It is the Man Who Was a Windsinger," said one. "He is dead."

"I myself looked at him lying on the desert," said another. "Though I came not near, I saw him there. He was dead."

They stood terror stricken. In the silence the fluttering of a flame sounded clearly.

One lifted the blanket over the door and looked out. The others followed him, huddled close in the darkness. No horse and rider could they see. Windsinger was gone.

"He rode my horse away. See—I had him tied under that cedar, and he is not there."

By the light of a brand from the fire they looked at the trampled sand. Under the tree were naked footprints.

"He was dead, but we saw him here——"

"The gods killed him—and the gods have sent him back."

"They sent him with a warning to the People—"

"The water is rising, he said. The world will be covered with water."

"A flood as in the worlds below—"

"It happened there, and it can happen again."

"But how can we reach a hole in the sky?"

"He said to go to the mountains and the mesas—"

Their voices rose in confused terror and awe as they peered vainly into the darkness.

And across the desert rode a naked man who had taken the path of white lightning and found the gods.

He came to a place of drums and dancing, where men and women paced to a chant of war. In the light of the great fires he stood with a blanket wrapped about him against the cold of the night.

"Flee," he cried once more. "With your flocks and your herds, your silver and blankets, make haste to the high places of the earth. The waters are rising and the gods have spoken."

The drum faltered. The men and women stood still.

"It is Windsinger," murmured the crowd.

"Windsinger, who is dead!"

Already he was gone and by another fire was rousing the sleeping men and women.

"Awake! Awake! Sleep no more until you go to the tops of the mountains. For the waters are rising in all the places of the earth—"

Their startled faces looked toward the blanketed man, who stood bare legged and bare armed before them. Above his streaming hair one arm was raised in summons and on his arm a blackened silver bracelet hung.

"It is the Man Who Was a Windsinger. But one came from the cliffs of the mesa two days ago, and said that Windsinger was struck by the lightning of the gods."

His voice came back through the darkness as he

hurried toward the shelter where the women had been cooking all day long.

"I have been to the dwelling places of the gods and they have sent the warning—"

He stood in the shelter, dimly lighted with red coals.

"Go! Go from this place to the mountains. Flee before the great waters."

In the shadow the sleeping people moved. But the voice in the night was already gone. On a fresh horse Windsinger was riding hard through the dark.

Four old women standing together beside the great fire spoke in voices that quavered with age and excitement.

"When I was a young woman in my mother's hogan they said a child had been born, and lived, though the moon fainted. When he was a man he became a Windsinger."

"He was marked by the gods at his birth."

"I remember they said he would be killed by the divine ones in their anger."

"That, or go some day to the hogans of the gods—"

The drums were silent and the chanting was done. Already men were saddling their horses, and riding away.

"I will go and round up my horses," said one. "This thing is true perhaps."

When the dawn came they were far from that place, riding homeward against the adobe rim of day.

※ ※

Windsinger reached the Tsagi while it still held the cold light of early morning. When the sun swung out at last into the narrow band of blue above him, he had nearly reached the hogan where lived the Clear-eyed One.

He had lost his blanket and rode once more naked. With a whip of sage he urged his weary horse to a faster pace. When he passed the sheep that his sons were driving to the foot of the canyon, the boys looked at him and fled. But Windsinger pressed on.

The Clear-eyed One saw him coming afar off, but she did not flee or show alarm. Quietly she waited for him to come near. Quietly then she spoke to him.

"They told me you were dead, struck by lightning from the sky."

"Not dead, my wife, but alive—and the gods have spoken to me."

Wearily she turned away.

"You went then to the hogans of the gods?"

The cool scorn in her voice brought no pain this time to the prophet.

"I have been to the hogans of the gods, and from them I have brought a warning to the People. The waters are rising and the earth will be covered. From end to end of the desert the People are preparing for flight."

The Clear-eyed One looked at him with pity as she answered him.

"You are tired. Sleep now, and you will see the truth."

Windsinger seemed not to hear her.

"Come," he cried. "We too must go. I have ridden hard since day to save you from the flood."

"You are tired," she said again. "I have food ready, and the chao is cool and waiting."

She took him into the chao, and brought him clothing—

"For you have come home naked from the place of the gods," she said.

She set food before him—

"Did the gods feed you?" she asked.

But her face was kind when she saw him suddenly asleep. She went outside, and unsaddled the horse, sending him with a sharp blow of the sage whip to water and to grass.

She called to her sons, who had brought their

sheep back up the canyon, and were standing at a distance fearfully.

"Your father is here. He was not dead."

Then she sat down at her loom and worked as if there were no strangeness in the morning.

The shadow of the western side of the canyon had climbed the eastern cliffs when Windsinger awoke.

"I have slept," he cried. "I have slept when I should be carrying the warning of the gods."

The Clear-eyed One looked up in concern as he ran out of the chao.

"You still speak of seeing the gods. For a lifetime you have dreamed. I will not listen."

He looked at her with eyes that saw the splendor of hogans built of black water and wind—

"I have gone that way," he said. "I have had white lightning flung out for my feet, and Hast-seyalti has led me there."

The Clear-eyed One was silent.

"We will have a singer," she said at last. "He will chant the songs of the Rock Crystal Boy and the Rock Crystal Girl, who dwell in the mountain of white daylight and gave men minds."

"You speak words that are foolishness, my wife. Always you have seen clearly save in this thing. Now you must listen to me. The gods have spoken, and I speak in their place to you. The waters are rising, and will cover the earth."

"What god has spoken?" she asked.

"Hastseyalti, who led me on the path of lightning; Hastsehogan, who came to meet us; Water Sprinkler, whose jar of all waters holds none strong enough to stop this flood. Even greater gods have spoken; the Woman Who Rejuvenates Herself, and her son, Slayer of the Alien Gods; the White Shell Woman also, and Child of the Waters. All these have I seen. All these have spoken."

The wind rustled in the aspens. The Clear-eyed One was silent.

"The day is nearly gone," said Windsinger then. "Even now our son comes up the canyon. You will ride together, driving the flock to the mesa. And I, who have slept when the gods would send a warning to the People,—I will go alone and take the word to every hogan of the desert."

The boys with the sheep came near. The flock was around them.

"Bring horses," called Windsinger. "Horses for each of us, my sons."

The Clear-eyed One hesitated, then turned away.

"Bring no horse for me," she said.

Windsinger followed her.

"You speak foolishness in this thing," he said

again. "The People are making ready. Will you alone stay behind?"

"I will stay behind," she said.

They stood facing each other—the Clear-eyed One with her lined strong face, Windsinger with his hair still straggling and unbound, his whole being intent upon his warning.

The fire went slowly out of his face.

"Then I stay also," he said.

The Clear-eyed One came to him swiftly.

"Now you know that you have dreamed this thing."

He shook his head.

"I have been to the dwelling place of the holy ones," he said slowly. "I speak the truth which they have spoken to me. But a long time ago I rode away from this canyon, because you told me to go; and I found that I did not want to live alone. I do not want to live, if you stay here and the waters cover you."

He went heavily into the hogan and lay down on his sheepskins. The Clear-eyed One built a fire and began to prepare their meal.

"Come," she said at last. "Here is food, hot and waiting."

But Windsinger did not come. She brought tea in a tin cup, and a tortilla fried to a golden brown.

"Here is food," she repeated.

Windsinger did not turn when the food was placed on the ground beside him. The Clear-eyed One and her sons ate their meal in silence.

Then suddenly Windsinger came out. Once more his face was aflame.

"Shall I fail in the task the gods have given me?" he cried. "Though I die, and the waters cover my wife and my sons, yet must I take the warning to the People. The gods have commanded me."

He turned to his older son.

"Bring my horse," he ordered him. "I must travel far tonight."

He spoke with authority. The boy, unprotesting, hurried away.

Windsinger drank the hot tea and ate the tortilla.

"I will take the warning to the People, and then I will come back. I meant what I said. I will not go without you to the mountain."

They sat for a long time in silence. Windsinger stared at the fire while his wife watched him, wondering.

"Your bracelets are black," she said at last.

He held out his arms and looked at them.

"I have been on a long journey," he replied. "They tarnished on the way."

Once more they waited silently. Finally the boy came back leading a horse by a rope. Windsinger saddled him and mounted.

"Perhaps yet you will hear the warning of the gods," he said. "For surely the waters are rising and will cover the earth."

The Clear-eyed One watched him until a turn in the canyon hid him from sight. Then she turned and spoke slowly to her sons.

"We will drive the sheep in the morning out into the Pass, for long ago men traveled on lightning to the gods, and in the worlds below the waters rose. Perhaps there is truth in this thing. . . ."

Once more the prophet rode upon the desert, crying his warning to the People.

"Make haste to the high places. The waters are rising."

They heard him in the valley of great rocks beyond Agathla. When he had carried his warning there, he turned back, past the dark height of Agathla, past the long red ridge, until he came to Dinnehotso, the Meadows of the People.

"I have gone on white lightning to the dwelling places of the gods," he cried. "From them I bring the warning. All the waters of the earth are rising. The land will be covered."

From the Meadows of the People he rode to the far blue cliffs of the mesa.

Through days and nights of desperate haste he followed the cliffs, until on that slope of piñon and cedar, and down on the sunbaked desert, the People made ready for flight. To Chilchinbito, to the hogans near the monastery of those who taught the white man's faith, to Chinli and the Canyon de Chelly, the stronghold of the People and the gods, to all the People dwelling in the low places of the desert, the prophet went. He cried his warning at the trading posts where men and women were gathered together. He came at last even to the agency in the town of green cottonwoods. To the white traders and the farmers he gave the word from the desert gods, heeding not their laughter when they turned away, pitying them when they could not understand.

"Truly the gods told me this thing," he said. "On the surface of the earth will come all waters: melted snow and hail, rain water, water from all springs and rivers and lakes, even the great water from the west where Day Bearer goes at night."

He sought out the Mender of Windmills.

"Now can I repay the debt of life I owe," he said. "To you who saved me at my birth, I bring this message from the holy ones."

The Mender of Windmills did not laugh as had the others of his race.

"But because we are friends, and speak truth to each other, I tell you that I cannot think this thing will come to pass," he said. "I stay here and do not flee from the waters."

Windsinger turned away sadly. Then once more he came back.

"Promise me one thing," he said, "because we are friends. When you see the water rising in the wells, wait not until the flood is upon you. But flee then to the high places."

The Mender of Windmills agreed.

"This thing I promise," he said.

Standing beneath the windmill, he watched Windsinger ride away.

But though the warning of the desert gods fell without conviction on the ears of an alien race, the desert people heard and believed.

"I myself saw this man lying on the ground dead," said the Son of the Eagle. "When I heard he had been seen alive, I went back to the place where he had been lying. I tell you he was gone. He died, and went to the gods, and came back again to warn us."

"It was said long ago that he would go to the dwelling places of the holy ones," said the old men.

"They wanted him at his birth; for the moon fainted."

"Some said the gods were angry then, and they scorned the ones who let him live. . . ."

"But some said that he would go like those others in old times and bring back songs from the holy ones."

They spoke also of those other floods, in the red world and in the black and white world, when the People had been driven up through the sky by the waters that covered all things.

"Perhaps even the mountains will not be high enough. Perhaps once more we will go up through the sky."

"But how shall we climb so high?"

"The holy ones will speak to us, and tell us how. Perhaps already they have explained to Windsinger, and he will tell us what to do when the waters cover the mountains."

"Was it not the Wind People who showed those others the way?"

Thus spoke the People, when the prophet had passed. They sent swift messengers to the distant canyons, that those of their family and clan might not be left to perish in the flood. When Windsinger passed at last the springs of Bakoshibito and came again to the mouth of the Tsagi, the warning had spread to every part of the desert, and already the flocks of the People were moving.

In the Pass he found the Clear-eyed One and their youngest son.

"I have come back," he told her. "We will die together beneath the great waters."

The Clear-eyed One spoke with humility.

"I will go with you to the mountain. I believe now that you have spoken the truth, and have brought this message from the holy ones."

Side by side they rode, driving their flock to the mesa. Their cattle also they took with them, their horses, and all their wealth in silver and turquoise and blankets of fine weaving.

In the country between the sacred mountains all the People were fleeing also, moving from the low places of the desert up the steep trails of the mountains and the mesas to safety.

The white men who lived among them remembered then the prophet whom they had scorned.

"It is that man who started the flight," they said. "What does he expect to get out of it?"

But the People said,

"He has been to the hogans of the gods and back again. He speaks the truth."

The farmer pleaded with them.

"What of your cornfields? Will you leave them when the corn is already tall and green?"

"Shall we lose our lives to save our corn?" they asked him.

Helpless he watched them pass—flock after flock of sheep and goats moving with the tinkle of little bells by night and day, herd after herd of cattle already beginning to fatten after the rain.

The traders also argued unavailingly.

"It is summer," they said. "White people will buy your goods. Will you carry all away?"

"Whatever we leave will be lost beneath the great waters," was the reply.

Steadily the march of the People went on.

A missionary labored among them.

"He brings you a false message," he said. "This prophet of yours speaks with a lying tongue, for he could not have seen gods which do not exist, nor can any flood cover the earth."

"He has seen the gods, and they have spoken," was the reply. "Have you not told us of a flood which your god sent?"

Still under blazing noons the flocks of the People moved. At night when the hot wind had died, and the desert chill returned, campfires blazed in places which before had been dark, and which another night would find dark again.

The young farmer at Todenestya appealed to the Mender of Windmills.

"A whole season's crops wasted!" he exclaimed. "Think of it, Matthew. Their cornfields ready for harvest, and left as if they'd never been planted."

The Mender of Windmills smiled gently.

"They've left their own cornfields," he said.

"But I'm responsible for them," said the farmer. "What'll I say in my report?"

"You'll have to say they were threatened with flood," chuckled the Mender of Windmills.

"A flood in the desert! You know this fellow who started it, don't you?"

"He's a friend of mine," said the Mender of Windmills.

"Go talk to him then. Get him off this business. What's he after anyway?"

"Nothing."

"Then what's the idea?"

"He has always walked with gods," said the Mender of Windmills.

The farmer started to laugh, and then stopped suddenly.

"You sound as if you believed him yourself," he exclaimed.

"No," admitted the Mender of Windmills. "In fact, I told him I didn't."

"You told him! Then you have talked to him already."

"A little," said the Mender of Windmills.

"Go talk to him again," insisted the farmer. "Think of the losses these people will suffer on account of him."

The Mender of Windmills considered.

"I'll try to see him," he agreed.

He found him, after much seeking. At the foot of the cliffs he was camped with the Clear-eyed One.

"I am glad, my friend," said Windsinger. "Now you too will be saved from the great waters. Is the water in the wells already rising?"

The Mender of Windmills dismounted.

"No, the water is not rising," he said. "I have come because the farmer at Todenestya has asked me to."

That night he sat by the fire with Windsinger and the Clear-eyed One. Not far away had burned that other fire to which he had come long ago when the moon fainted. Now he was bent, and his face was filled with kindly wrinkles, but once more he spoke the white man's wisdom.

"The mountains stretch between us and the great waters," he told Windsinger. "The waters cannot break through."

"Even over the mountains the water can come, if the gods will it so," said Windsinger.

The Mender of Windmills pondered.

"The gods seldom speak to men," he suggested.

Windsinger agreed.

"Seldom, my friend. But they have spoken to me."

The Mender of Windmills was silent. At last he spoke.

"When the gods speak, what can I say?" he asked. "For I am a man."

He wrapped himself in his blanket and slept. In the morning he bade farewell to Windsinger and rode away.

Still from the desert the People climbed to the slopes of piñon and cedar, and from the slopes of piñon and cedar up the steep trails to the high shade of aspen and pine.

The rich helped the poor, giving them horses to ride, and feeding them around their campfires at night.

As they fled they sought their friends.

"Do you know where the Son of Black Goat is? Has he passed this way?

"What of Burned Foot? Will he reach safety before the waters cover the land?"

They sought their kinsmen also.

"My father was to take this trail, but I cannot find him."

"Where is my elder brother who was to bring his horses here?"

So the People fled to the mountains and the mesas nearest them. And many came up the steep trails of Zilhlejini where Windsinger was, because its cliffs stretched gray for many miles, and on its height there was much grass.

III

WHEN they had come to Zilhlejini, they questioned Windsinger.

"When do the waters rise and cover the earth?"

"I only know what the gods told me," he answered them, "that swiftly we should go to the high places, for the waters are rising. Soon the waters will come."

From the cliffs of the mesa they looked out to the far edge of the desert day. Parched and brown the distances stretched before them; and the mountains far away were blue with summer.

"Soon we shall see the thin line of white," they said. "White water coming from north and east; white water coming from south and west. Like mountains stretching all around, the water will march on. So it did in the worlds below."

But day after day the distant mountains were blue with summer haze.

Some began to build hogans.

"We know not when the flood will come," they said. "Perhaps we shall be here for a long time. It is well that we have dwelling places."

They built chaos of green boughs cut from juniper and piñon and pine. Some built hogans of stout logs and earth. But others said,

"We shall build no dwelling places. For when the water comes who knows that even here we shall be high enough? In the worlds below, when the People had wings and bodies like those of the Grasshopper People, they had to fly up to the very sky to escape the white wave of water. They had to fly through the sky."

Then those who had built hogans in which to live said again,

"How shall we fly through the sky, if the water covers even this place?"

"Windsinger will tell us how."

They came to Windsinger and asked him this also. And Windsinger was troubled.

"The gods did not speak to me of this," he said. "Perhaps they will speak again."

He listened for their voices in the dawn and in the dusk. At last he said,

"In the worlds below the People did not know what they should do until the time was at hand. They touched the hard sky before they found the opening. We also will wait. When it is time, the gods will speak."

The People were content with that.

"Windsinger's words are wise," they said. "It is not strange that the gods have spoken to him."

Still those that were sick came to him for song; and days and nights of song passed by.

"There is grass here, but our flocks are many," said Windsinger at last. "It is time for us to go by families and by clans across the mesa, so that we shall have grass enough for all."

Again the People knew that he spoke wisdom. With their flocks they went great distances over the mesa until they met those who were coming from the other side. Riding among them, Windsinger allotted grazing places. Then those who had been living on the mesa were troubled.

"Our flocks have grazed here since long ago," they said. "How will so many find grass? Shall our sheep die?"

But Windsinger said,

"These others have fled for safety from the great waters. Where else will they go? Where else will they find grazing places?"

"It is true," they granted. "The gods have sent them, and we shall not grudge them grass."

So the flocks found food; and the People looked always to Windsinger for wisdom and for song.

Always on the cliffs of the mesa there were men looking for the far white wave. North and south and east and west the watchers were stationed. Day and night they scanned the horizon. But still the sun blazed upon parched distances; still the stars burned in night-blue skies.

"Even the rains have ceased," said the watchers. "The earth is dry."

"But not as rain will the flood come; as mountains of water marching—so will it come."

Still they waited, for mountain ranges marching white upon them. Still their flocks grazed upon the mesa.

At last the rains came again—dark rains that hung in light afar off. From the mesa the People watched.

"It is raining now around Agathla," said those who lived near that misted height of rock. "Soon grass will spring up there."

On another day those who lived at Dinnehotso rejoiced.

"Now it rains on the Meadows of the People," they said.

Sometimes lightning flashed in those distant storms.

"So it was when I took the way of white lightning to the gods," said Windsinger.

But though rain fell upon the desert, no high wave came marching from the edge of earth and sky. Day and night the People watched for it in vain.

At last they looked out upon the desert and saw that it was green.

"Grass has grown at Dinnehotso," they said.

"There is grass also around Agathla."

"There our flocks would find grazing places."

The word went back from the cliffs to the others who had taken refuge on that height of piñon and juniper and pine.

"There is grass down there upon the desert. And here our flocks are many; soon there will be nothing for them to eat."

Again they went to Windsinger.

"Tell us when the great waters will come. Tell us how long we must stay here upon the mesa."

But again Windsinger could say to them only what the gods had said to him.

"Soon the waters will rise. Soon the earth will be covered."

They went away. But from the cliffs they looked out over the leagues of light, and saw the desert green.

So the days passed, and the People dwelt still upon the mesa. At last their restlessness increased.

"Perhaps the gods have changed their minds. Perhaps the flood will not come," said one.

"Be careful how you speak, lest the holy ones hear you," reproved another.

But the whisper went from family to family, and around their hogan fires more and more of them said,

"Perhaps the flood will not come."

The old men spoke with careful wisdom.

"In the worlds below the white wave came. We know that from this world also some time we must fly upward. Now the gods have warned us to make ready. Let us not hastily go down again upon the desert. For the gods have spoken."

But day after day the watchers searched the far line of desert and sky; and always they said to the questioning people,

"We see no flood, nor any sign of a white wave coming. Only dark showers of rain sometimes, and the desert growing green."

Another whisper went swiftly across the mesa.

"Perhaps the gods did not speak."

The People questioned openly now, and argued among themselves.

"Would Windsinger lie? Always he has spoken truth to us."

"Always he has come to us with help, singing even for those who have neither silver nor sheep. Now would he drive us from our grazing places

with all our flocks and cattle if the gods had not
spoken?"

But while some argued thus, others said,

"For many days we have been here upon the
mesa, and the waters have not risen."

"Our grass here is growing scarce. Down there
upon the desert the rains have come, and there is
grass for our sheep."

"Shall we stay here waiting for a flood till Old
Age kills us all?"

Now even the old men murmured,

"Windsinger was ever a dreamer."

Once more they came to him.

"How long shall we stay here upon the mesa,
when our flocks need grass and the desert below us
is green? How long shall we wait for the waters to
rise?"

Again Windsinger said to them,

"I know only that the gods have warned us to
make haste to the high places. They would not have
spoken so, if the time were long."

"Have the gods indeed spoken so?" persisted one.

"I have told you," he answered them. "I have not
lied."

"What gods did you see?" they asked.

Again Windsinger told them.

"Hastseyalti, god of dawn; Hastsehogan, god of

evening; Black God, with his back to his fire; Water Sprinkler with his jar of all waters. These have I seen, and many other holy ones, when I took the path of white lightning to their dwelling places."

"Where did that path go?"

"Over the canyons and cliffs and mountains, over sand and rock and wide green places—I cannot tell you where it went, save that the gods were at its end."

Again they went away.

"He speaks like one who does not lie," they said. "He names the holy ones."

"Yet where is the flood?"

Still the watchers from the cliffs looked out over distances of shadow and sun. Heights of dark rock and barriers of far blue mountains were there. Below them sometimes an eagle circled. And the desert was green.

At last there were few to speak in Windsinger's defense when men said of him,

"He is a dreamer."

"When he was born, the old men said he should have been killed."

"If he has gone indeed on the path of white lightning, he learned witchcraft, and not the ways of the gods."

Finally one family came to the cliffs and looked out over the grass that stretched below them.

"Shall our sheep grow lean in this place where the flocks of the People are so many, and the grass is nearly gone? Down there our flocks will find food enough. Let us go."

And down the steep trail from the mesa they went with their sheep and their cattle back to the desert.

The Son of the Eagle came to Windsinger and brought him word of this.

"The others murmur also, and are making ready to go," he said.

Windsinger rode to the cliff and waited at the place where the trail plunged downward. When others came that way, they found him there.

"We go back to our own hogans," they said. "The waters will not rise."

"The gods have spoken and the gods do not lie," said Windsinger.

"The gods may have spoken; but they set no time for the flood. Old Age may kill many times before it comes. Our sons and our sons' sons may not live to see it. Shall we live forever here on the mesa?"

They passed him, driving their sheep and goats and cattle down the trail.

Then Windsinger sent forth swift runners to all those who had come from the desert to the mesa.

"Send men to hear me speak of this thing," he said. "Let me tell you the words of the gods."

Some said,

"He has told us many times what the gods said. Shall we listen again?"

And they stayed away. But others rode to Windsinger's hogan and said,

"We have listened to you, for we believed that you had taken the way to the gods. We will listen to you once more. We are willing to hear, if you have some new thing to say."

Then Windsinger, astride his horse, spoke to them.

"Since I was a child I have lived among you, and you know me," he said. "There are old men who can still remember when I was born, and how the moon fainted. There are many who can remember how I tended sheep on the desert, the sheep that my mother owned until the winter when many died in the hogans of the People. You know that even in those days I dealt fairly. I did not lie."

"That is true," granted those who listened.

"When I was a young man I learned the songs of the Wind Chant; and after that the old men taught me other chants also. I came to you when you sent for me; I came even when you had no sheep and no silver. I took from you only small gifts, that the command of the gods might not go unheeded and healing be won without payment. A loaf of bread sometimes, a single goatskin—such payment I took, and said that it was enough. You know that I speak truth."

"You speak truth," they granted.

"You sent for me often to settle your disputes. I was judge, and I judged fairly. Again you know that I speak truth."

"It is so," they agreed.

"Hear me when I speak to you now, and know that once more I speak truth. I tell you what I have not told you before. Old men and old women among you can remember that at my birth the moon fainted; the gods thought then of me. Through the years of my life I have known that they were near. I have known that I walked with gods. I did not see them, and though I listened for their call in the morning and at night, I could not hear their voice. Yet always I knew that they had chosen me for a task such as men in old times have performed. I knew that I should go to their dwelling place and bring back songs to the People. At last I went singing to the house of the Old People, and sought the gods there. They did not come to me; they did not speak; but they showed me a path of white light in the sky, and I knew I should walk upon it. Yet because they did not come then, and because they did not speak, I was heavy hearted. I thought they laughed at me for seeking them; I thought they scorned the boy who had learned their songs, the man who had chanted for the People."

His voice was low with feeling as the slow phrases came. They listened and were silent.

"I rode that night across the desert," he continued. "The first rain had come, and the Lightning People and the Thunder People were there. I rode with a heavy heart. Then swiftly the white light came again, a path of white lightning in the night. On it I went to the gods."

"You have told us this," murmured some.

"They gave me no songs. They gave me no sand paintings. But they spoke to me. I have told you their names. I speak them again: Talking God of Dawn, House God of Evening, Black God of Fire, Water Sprinkler; the mighty ones also—the Woman Who Rejuvenates Herself, and Slayer of the Alien Gods. They gave me a task that was greater than singing—the task of saving the People from death. They told me of waters rising in flood as in the worlds below they had risen. They told me to carry the word to the People, and warn them to go to the mountains and the mesas. 'For this task you were born; for this task you have waited. Go now, for you have heard the gods speak.' This the holy ones said to me when I found them in their dwelling places.

"I heard them, and then again I was on the desert. It was night. I saw that my clothing had worn out on the journey and I was naked. I saw that my silver was black, so far had I gone to find the gods. Already perhaps the waters were rising, and the gods had sent me to warn the People. I went swiftly, as they had commanded. I carried the word to the distant places of the desert. And the People fled. You heard me then and fled with the others. Hear me now.

"Will you throw away the safety you have found? Will you go down from this mountain to the desert? Will you defy the command of the gods? You are safe here from the great waters. Your wives are safe. Your children are safe. All your sheep and goats and horses and cattle you have brought from places which soon will be underneath the water. Will you take them down again to the desert and lose them all? Will you take your wives, your sons, and your daughters down again to the low places to die together, so that again the gods

will have to make new men and women out of corn
and wind?

"Hear me! I have spoken truth to you through
the years of my life. Now old age is near me. Still I
speak truth!"

The people were quiet.

"But where is the great water upon the desert?"
one asked at last.

"How long shall we wait?" demanded another.

"The grass on the desert is green after the rains,"
said a third.

And they went back to their families and their
flocks.

In the morning they started down the steep trails.
Little herdboys driving their sheep and goats; old
men with white hair tied in bright headbands; old
women with the strong sure faces of those who
managed many flocks; young men riding arrogantly
with laughter and mocking talk of floods; young
women with their baby boards on their backs—
all rode down from the mesa along the trails they
had climbed in terror and in haste.

From morning until night for many days the
march went on. By families and by clans the People
moved with all their flocks and herds.

Windsinger watched them go.

He stood at last upon the cliffs of Zilhlejini alone.

Below him on the desert the last of the flocks were moving slowly, creeping slowly as water might creep along the ground. The last of the desert people had gone down from the mesa, and left the prophet alone.

He stood there silently. The light lengthened on the desert until the yellow evening came. A little wind breathed through sage and juniper. In the dusk he began to sing. His low song beat in the silence, and ended with the coming of the dark.

Then the Clear-eyed One came to him.

"I have food ready," she said. "Come, for it is night."

He turned to her. In the dim light his face was tired and old.

"Let us stay here," he said, "here upon the mesa. The gods do not lie."

"It is well," said the Clear-eyed One. "Together we will stay upon the mesa."

And she led him to the fire, where there was food and rest.

IV. THE BLACK WIND

It was night, and from the north the black wind blew.

I

A T last Windsinger also came down from the mesa to the desert.

He came with a heavy heart.

"But the People spoke truly," he said. "The white wave has not come. Who knows when the gods will send it?"

The Clear-eyed One came with him, and their sons drove the sheep and goats down the steep trail. So they came once more to the slope at the foot of the gray cliffs.

"We will stay here," said Windsinger then. "Here I was born, and here in my childhood I herded sheep. Here perhaps I may find the gods again."

At the foot of the gray cliffs they built their hogan, and their sheep grazed there.

Those who rode that way stopped sometimes and spoke to them.

"You too have come down from the mesa," they said to Windsinger. "Have you decided after all that the gods spoke falsely?"

"The gods speak truth," he said simply.

"Then what of the white wave, and the rising waters? Did not the gods tell you of that?"

Windsinger looked at them sadly.

"I do not know," he said.

His son asked him for songs.

"Teach me more songs of the Wind Chant," he begged.

"Do not ask me to sing for a little while," Windsinger replied.

"But sometime you will teach me songs again, so that I too may be a singer?"

"I will teach you the rest of the Wind Chant when there is song in me once more."

"And the new songs of the gods?"

"Them I know not," said Windsinger.

The Clear-eyed One spoke no more to him of the gods nor of the waters rising. But always she was near him, moving with kindness to give him food, to spread sheepskins when he was weary, to send away those who came with mockery.

"Soon you will walk again in the trail of peace," she said. "Yes, you will sing again."

But now no one came to their hogan asking him to sing. Even those upon whom he had looked with pity and to whom he had given his songs for a loaf of bread sent now for other singers.

"Sleepy Singer will lead the Wind Chant for the wife of Nasja," Windsinger told the Clear-eyed One. "Once I would have gone to their hogan."

"Another time they will come for you," com- forted the Clear-eyed One.

She rode away one day to the trading post with goatskins and wool. When she returned she brought word of an Entah.

"The last day they will come to the Pass," she said. "They have chosen a place near the mouth of the Tsagi."

"You would see those of your own family there," said Windsinger.

"Yes, they will be there."

Windsinger was silent. The Clear-eyed One sat down before her loom.

"We will go together to the Entah," said Wind- singer at last.

When the day came they left their sons to care for the sheep and rode over the desert. Windsinger had gone that way to an Entah before, and had met the girl whose eyes were like rock crystal. Now though she rode beside him straight and strong and clear-eyed still, the years had lined her face with sadness. Now he too was old, and the song had fled.

They passed the trading post. Windsinger thought of the traders who had come and gone since the half-breed had watched him herding his sheep as a child. As they climbed the hill past the farmer's house he remembered the farmers who had come to plant green fields since the day he had seen a woman weep at the sight of a blue heron in a strange land. Some had come with wives and children; some had come alone, like that young man who had begged the People to stay their flight from the great waters. They had briefly shared the life of the desert people and had gone away. Yet still over the desert the flocks of the People drifted. . . .

Yonder behind the high-pitched rocks of the red ridge the dark shaft of Agathla lifted, unchanging. The mesa, dark always as if the shadow of a cloud were on it, stood as if the gods had sprinkled it with pollen, and peace were there. The permanence of it came to him with a sense of peace in his own heart. He felt himself again a part of life and earth, who had felt himself cut off.

The Son of the Eagle with his wife and sons joined them as they rode into the Pass. Windsinger greeted him with hesitancy, wondering if they would speak mocking words to him as had those others who had come to his hogan. They spoke instead with friendliness, and in friendliness they all rode on together.

Nevertheless, when they came at last to the place of the Entah, Windsinger knew again the bitterness of the People's scorn. They laughed at him when they saw him coming.

"Here comes Windsinger," they said, "the man who said he had talked with gods."

"Here is the prophet of the flood. Perhaps he has found an arroyo where water runs."

As he and the Clear-eyed One watched the morning ceremony, none of the mounted men and women turned to them. Alone in all that crowd of desert people they sat apart, watching the girl with the staff of war lead the procession of women, listening to the beat of drum and song which sounded from the hogan near at hand.

When the morning ceremony was over, the Clear-eyed One sought her own people and Windsinger went alone to the shelter where the great fires were burning under the pots of mutton and beef.

As he lifted the blanket over the door and stepped into the flecked dimness of the interior, again the people turned to him.

"Will you warn us of another flood?" asked one.

"Have you walked again on a path of white lightning?" demanded another.

The others laughed. One old man turned to them with reproof.

"This is not the way of peace fitting for an Entah. Let your thought hold no bitterness."

Then they were silent and spoke no more of

Windsinger. But when he had taken food and sat down to eat it, he found himself alone. No man gave him news of rains in distant places of the desert, nor of sickness in the hogans of the People. No man said to him,

"Come to my hogan and sing."

He ate the food and went out. Under a piñon he sat alone and looked across the Pass to the red cliffs of the Tsagi. People came and went. In the distance small fires were sending up smoke, and in the shade men and women rested and slept. The sun sank lower in the west.

At dusk when the drums began again and the girl with the staff came out to choose her partner for the first hour of dancing, he drifted with the rest to the place of the dance. The song lifted in the yellow twilight, and in the song he felt again that he was taking up the broken threads of his life. This had been and still would be—this song like the familiar height of mountain and mesa.

But though song called him, he stood apart from these people who did not want him near. He watched the dancing, and when it was over went again to the shelter and ate.

In the evening when the great fires were lighted and again the girl with the staff came forth to lead the dancers, the Clear-eyed One sat beside him.

Once she had carried the staff of war, and the people when he passed had pointed him out as the man she had chosen. . . .

As the night wore on and the smoke rose, yellowed with firelight, to the dark sky, he lived again that Entah of his youth, finding a certain happiness in the memory of happiness.

Song and firelight and the shuffle of pacing feet in the sand; the beat of the drum and the clinking of silver girdles—all at last was done.

"Let us go now," said Windsinger to the Clear-eyed One.

Before the coming day was more than a half dreamed light in the eastern sky, they rode away. When full day came, cutting the buttes and mesas from darkness, they were alone on the trail, far from the place of song.

After the Entah Windsinger began again to teach his son the songs of the Wind Chant, and in them found a certain peace as in lasting things. But he went no more to the ceremonies of the desert people, for the scorn of those who had been his friends was sharp in his heart.

Sometimes a little herdboy or a herdgirl rode by with sheep. Sometimes a woman on her way to the trading post stopped for a few slow words with the

Clear-eyed One. Windsinger saw only these, who came and passed on.

"Come with me to the trading post," the Clear-eyed One suggested.

But at the trading post he found no more the old friendliness, and riding back to his hogan he was again sad.

So the months of wind and snow passed by, and summer blazed again upon the desert.

Early in the summer some white men came that way. For a little while they camped near Windsinger's hogan, and bought mutton from the Clear-eyed One. When Windsinger went to their camp they showed him fossils which they had gathered.

"They are hunting the bones of the Alien Gods that Day Bearer buried in the rocks," Windsinger told the Clear-eyed One when he returned.

At last even those who hunted the bones of the Alien Gods departed. At the foot of the mesa Windsinger and the Clear-eyed One were again alone.

Still in Windsinger's heart was a dull despair— the despair of a man who had sought the gods and been turned away. In him was the pain of an unanswered cry. Why, why had the flood not come? Why had the gods spoken and then betrayed him? As he sat long hours in the shade of the chao, gazing

at the chill blue shadow of the cliffs shearing away
into distances of light, he asked still another question: had the gods spoken; had he seen them in
their dwelling places?

Over and over again he made the journey of that
remembered night: riding in the rain from the
Tsagi, despairing of any word from the gods; riding
in the rain and thunder and lightning, until the
path of lightning stretched before him, and he heard
the gods speak. . . . Surely this could not have been
a dream, though they called him a dreamer. Surely
the gods had spoken.

But sitting there in the motionless immensity of
the desert, the question came again, not to be set
aside. Where was the flood, which the gods had said
would be? Had the gods, who spoke no falsehood,
spoken falsely to him? Or had the gods spoken?

To the question there came no answer, no call of
the holy ones, four times repeated. Silent the desert
lay under the blazing sky. Windsinger pondered
alone.

He was alone as he had not been even when he
rode away from the Tsagi and the Clear-eyed One.
Then he had despaired of a dream's fulfillment;
now the fulfillment had turned to bitterness. Again
the harsh doubt returned. Perhaps the gods had indeed laughed, mocking his dream with another

dream, because he had thought to find them in their dwelling places.

At such times he would call his elder son to him and teach him songs. Singing, he knew old peace.

※ ※

The Mender of Windmills came at last to Windsinger's hogan. Windsinger, seeing him while he was yet far away, shrank from the meeting.

"He told me that the waters would not rise," said Windsinger to the Clear-eyed One. "He followed me then even to the mesa to tell me so."

Slowly over the distances of light the wagon crawled. Up from the desert it came to the slope of piñon and cedar. Windsinger waited, fearing that his friend came with reproaches.

But when he looked into the face of the Mender of Windmills he was glad; and the Mender of Windmills spoke no word of the People's flight, but grasped Windsinger's hand in the old greeting.

"Yahteh, shi kiz—it is well, my friend."

That night he stayed in Windsinger's hogan and the Clear-eyed One set food before him.

"You are our friend. It is good that you are here," she said.

They sat talking beside the fire until late in the night.

"You do not ride over the desert as you once

did," the Mender of Windmills said to Windsinger. "Once I saw you often, as I came to the windmills. Now I do not see you."

Windsinger was silent.

"I go no longer to sing," he said at last. "No man sends for me."

The Mender of Windmills looked at him quickly. Then he too was silent. The fire blazed between them.

"I have come to ask you to sing," said the Mender of Windmills slowly. "Once your songs brought me health when I was sick. Now again I need them. I come seeking them."

Windsinger looked at him doubtfully.

"You are sick, my friend?"

The Mender of Windmills hesitated.

"I am old," he said.

Windsinger saw that it was so. Gray and bent, with a hand that shook with age, the Mender of Windmills sat opposite him in the firelight.

"When I was born, you were a man," granted Windsinger. "Now I too am old. And I have no songs to make us young again." He paused. "The Slayer of the Alien Gods did not slay Old Age. It is right that we grow old and die."

His low voice fell into silence. They sat in the firelight without speaking, and the Clear-eyed One came and sat beside them. In the shadow the two boys lay sleeping.

The Mender of Windmills was the first to speak.

"In my old age I have pain here in my hip, in my leg. It often troubles me. You have songs for such a pain?"

"I have songs for that pain," said Windsinger.

"Those songs I ask," said the Mender of Windmills. "Whatever chant you will—a one day chant, a nine day chant—I will be content."

Again they were silent. The fire burned low, and the desert quietness was around them.

"I will sing for you, my friend," said Windsinger.

On the day that had been set Windsinger rode down the slope of the mesa more nearly happy than he had been since he had seen the People turning back from their flight.

He passed the trading post where he could see a group of men point at him with laughter. He watered his horse at the windmill. Then on through the Pass he rode to the place of song.

They had built there a hogan, and already many were gathered waiting for him. They did not laugh as he came near. He came a singer, a priest of the wind rite.

The Mender of Windmills welcomed him gravely.

"I have made all things ready," he said. "If there is anything else, tell me and I will do it."

"You have done well," said Windsinger.

Once more he guided the making of the prayer sticks and men obeyed him. Once more he directed the designs of the sand painting, and according to his word it grew in beauty of color and line.

The old dignity of command was sweet to him. And sweet that night were the voices coming closer through the dark, as men came to join the rite of song.

The firelight flickered on the faces of the People, and lighted the grave countenance of the Mender of Windmills for whom the People's songs were to be sung.

But when the time of chanting came, Windsinger forgot the others. He forgot even the Mender of Windmills. As he sang, the gods were near.

The Clear-eyed One watched Windsinger ride up again from the low plains of light to the shaded slope of the mesa.

As he swung from his saddle she searched his face, and when she looked away there was content upon her own.

"It is well," she said.

"It is well," repeated Windsinger.

The seasons slipped by with sun and wind and snow, and sun again. On the slope of the mesa Windsinger remembered that for a little while the gods had been near him as he sang, near him as in the long ago.

In the memory was peace, and at last a new wondering.

"I have felt the holy ones near me. Perhaps yet I shall hear them speak, and speak with certainty."

For a little while he felt again the old tension of search and waiting, and the old despair when no call sounded upon the desert.

Then as he sat one day in the sunlight he thought of those others who had found the holy ones.

"They found the gods without searching," he said. "One was hunting when the Mountain Sheep People took him. To the beggar on the cliff the Eagles came. . . ."

He thought for a long time of these things. At last he said,

"I will search no longer, for my searching has not brought me to the holy ones. If they come to me, it is well. If not, that too is well."

He was sad, because at the end of his search he had not found the gods. But he knew rest, as if after riding a long trail he had come at last to the shade of green trees.

❧ ❧

His elder son came to him and said,

"A man has asked me to sing for his grandmother, who is sick."

"Go, my son," said Windsinger. "You have learned the songs of the Wind Chant and are ready."

After that men came often to the slope of the mesa asking for the son of Windsinger. And Windsinger watched his son ride forth to sing.

"Soon," said the Clear-eyed One, "our elder son will take a wife, and go away from us."

At last he came to them, saying,

"I have found a woman whom I want for my wife."

When they had heard her name and her clan they gave him sheep and cows and turquoise, and he rode away.

Then Windsinger and the Clear-eyed One had only their younger son.

"Soon he too will go," said the Clear-eyed One.

❧ ❧

The Mender of Windmills came sometimes to the hogan at the foot of the mesa. He and Windsinger sat together beside the fire, and were often silent.

"The next time I come, I will have a boy with me," said the Mender of Windmills on one of his trips. "I have gone from windmill to windmill alone for many years; but now that I am old, I need help."

Windsinger agreed quietly.

"You will take a boy of the People?"

"Yes," said the Mender of Windmills. "A boy of the People to help me on the People's windmills."

They looked into the fire and were silent again.

Still the seasons passed, with slender winds and big winds, with light woman-rain and heavy man-rain, with planting and ripening of the desert corn.

At last Windsinger and the Clear-eyed One were alone in their hogan at the foot of the mesa, for their younger son also had taken a wife and had gone to live with her people and her clan.

Now the Clear-eyed One took the sheep forth in the morning and brought them home again at night. Like the drifting of smoke, like the flowing of slow water, her flock moved on the desert. At the windmills and the trading post the desert people spoke to her with respect as one of age and dignity.

She brought word to Windsinger of an Entah.

"Again they come near us for the last day's ceremony," she said. "Let us go."

Windsinger did not protest. Again they rode to an Entah together.

Beside the small fires in the shelter where the

mutton and coffee boiled, beside the great fires
lighted for the dance of war, Windsinger sat once
more. The people with the passing of time had forgotten to laugh at him, and he moved almost un-
noticed among them.

Again he heard with deep content the old throb
of song, and watched the dancers moving back and
forth in the firelight, with the clinking of bracelets and the shuffle of pacing feet. The Clear-eyed
One was beside him through the long night of song
and flame—the Clear-eyed One, who had danced
once that slow measure, carrying the staff of
war. . . .

At dawn they rode away, and others rode with
them along the trail.

So in the slow march of days Windsinger found
a certain quietness. The People had ceased to laugh
at him. And song had come again with healing. . . .

He sat in the shade of the chao, watching the
drift of sheep as the Clear-eyed One moved with
her flock in the distance. Immense with light and
stillness, the morning held the desert. From the
height of the mesa to the dark shaft of Agathla,
all things shared the clarity of day. . . .

For a long time he sat there; suddenly he became
aware of the wide light of the morning, of the

stillness of earth and sky. Aware of it, a part of it, he sat motionless.

As if he had been a tree uprooted, he felt the roots of his being strike again into the desert earth, part of its wind and light, part of its rock and sand, part of its waiting silence.

He knew the desert as he had known it when as a boy he stood in the starlit wind of night. He knew it as he had with his sheep, moving in the poised desert noon.

But he did not look back to those brief sensings of earth. In this moment all his being paused.

As surely as if he had heard their call, he felt the desert gods near. . . .

Now there was no tension of seeking, no despair of an abandoned quest. He did not look to see their faces; he did not harken for their call.

But on the desert he knew the gods were moving: Day Bearer, robed in morning light; Slayer of the Alien Gods, striding valiant on butte and mountain range; The Woman Who Rejuvenates Herself, moving with divinity in all life and growth. . . .

In that moment of knowledge there was no memory of fainting moon, nor white light in the north; there was no desire for a bridge of lightning to the hogans of the holy ones. For the holy ones were there.

There in the wide light of the morning, in the breathing of desert earth. There without voice as in the Night Chant, or body as in the sand paintings. Unheard and unseen, but surely there, living and a part of life. . . .

Windsinger in that moment was still, sensing the breathing of mountain and desert. Into rock and piñon his spirit moved; he and the earth and the wind, and the wide light of morning were one, and one with the moving presence of the holy ones. . . .

The moment ended. In the distance the flock moved like a low cloud, wind driven. The piñons stirred in the spiced sharpness of day.

Windsinger sat still motionless in the shade of the green chao, and his voice sounded in low song.

II

WINDSINGER was old, and lay at last upon his sheepskins, helpless and ill.

"Send now for our elder son, that he may sing for me," he said to the Clear-eyed One.

And up the slope of the mesa, their elder son came to sing.

Now Windsinger stayed out of the hogan while a younger voice gave brief commands for the making of the sand painting—"Blue," "Yellow," "Black." He sat silent through the chanting and heard a younger voice carrying on from song to song. But he knew again the quietness of the chanted prayers, as he had known it singing. Quietness as the afternoon light slanted through the smokehole on the colored sands; quietness at evening as firelight flickered on the faces of the singers and song throbbed and fell into silence.

"Now all is peace; now all is peace. . . ."

So chanted the desert men.

"Now all is peace," murmured Windsinger. And his heart was at rest.

But when the chanting was done, and the Clear-eyed One went forth again with her flock, Wind-

singer still lay on his sheepskins. Days of sun blazed
upon the desert; nights of white starlight moved by.

"Not yet do I walk upon the trail of peace," said
Windsinger at last. "Perhaps it is the Path of Spirits
and not the Wind Chant which I need."

So once more there was song on the slope of the
mesa. The Clear-eyed One cooked food for those
who came; and Windsinger sat once more silent
through a chant which he had led in years gone by.
Again the songs fell upon him with old peace.

"Now I shall be well," he said. "Now all evil
has fled, and I walk the trail of peace."

But when the people were gone away, and the
singer also had departed, Windsinger still stayed in
his hogan.

"Not yet is there strength in my body," he said.

The Clear-eyed One was troubled as she herded
her sheep on the desert. When she came to the
windmills and there at the meeting place of the
desert trails spoke with others of the People, she
could only say to them,

"Twice have we held chants for my husband,
and still he is no better."

She spoke with the Mender of Windmills, and
when he heard that his friend was sick he went to
his hogan.

"I am older than you," said the Mender of Windmills. "When you were born I was a man. Yet still I take the road between the windmills. Soon you will be well again, and I shall see you riding on the desert."

"Soon perhaps I will find the chant that will make me strong again," agreed Windsinger.

But when at last the Mender of Windmills went away, he went with a sad heart.

"He is old, and I too am old," he said to the boy who rode beside him on the wagon. Then Windsinger's words came back to him, and he added, "The Slayer of the Alien Gods did not slay Old Age."

After that another white man rode to Windsinger's hogan. He explained through an interpreter that he was a doctor from the agency and that the Mender of Windmills had sent him. When he went away he left medicines, and Windsinger took them until they were gone. But still he lay sick.

"I have heard of a singer beyond the mesa who has great power," said the Clear-eyed One at last. "Let us send for him."

"Send for him," approved Windsinger.

Once more the People came to the slope of the mesa to join in the chanted prayers.

For nine days and nine nights the great rite continued, with the making of prayer wands and sand

paintings, with the chanting of songs in their order.
From great distances the people came; and as
they rode up the slope of the mesa they recalled
the days when Windsinger himself led the great
chants.

"Even for those who had no wealth in sheep and
silver, even for them he sang," they said.

And Windsinger, who remembered still their
scorn, felt their friendliness warm about him and
was glad.

Song, throbbing in desert sunlight, sounding still
in the piñon scented dark; desert men singing while
nine days and nine nights marched by; and at the
end of every prayer the sure refrain,

"Now all is peace, now all is peace."

The firelight flickered on Windsinger's face, lined
with age and pain. But strength also was there and
calm.

"Now all is peace, now all is peace."

The last song throbbed into silence. The last of
the singers rode away. Again Windsinger and the
Clear-eyed One were alone upon the slope of the
mesa.

Days of sun and nights of clear starlight; days
of heat and nights of sharp, still cold; then at last
the chill wind of winter coming. . .

"I have heard men tell of another singer," said the Clear-eyed One. "He can cure many kinds of sickness, they say."

"We have given sheep for many chants," said Windsinger. "It is enough."

When she rode forth with her sheep again, he called to her.

"Go this time to the trading post," he said. "Buy velvet and calico, and make clothing for me."

The swift pain on the face of the Clear-eyed One gave way to calm.

"Yahteh," she said. "I will go."

When she came again to the hogan at the foot of the mesa, she brought new velvet and calico, and made new clothes for Windsinger.

He called for them on a day of gray clouds when there was no sun upon the desert. A cold wind flapped the blanket which was hanging over the hogan door.

"Bring me now my clothing of new velvet and calico," he said to the Clear-eyed One. "Before Day Bearer brings light again to the world, I go to the yellow world of peace."

She brought him the clothes, and helped him as he put them on.

"Bring now my buckskin moccasins with the silver buttons," he said.

The Clear-eyed One brought these also.

"Now my silver and turquoise," commanded Windsinger. "I go not to the yellow world dressed like a slave."

The Clear-eyed One brought him his belt of heavy silver and he buckled it about his waist. She brought him his bracelets and he put them on his arms. She brought him his necklaces of silver and turquoise and coral, and he hung them around his neck.

"It is well," he said. "I go, a singer of the People."

In a voice that did not falter he began to sing.

Toward the cliffs of the mesa drove the Mender of Windmills. The gray day dimmed. . . .

"Tonight we will spend at Windsinger's hogan," he said to the boy beside him.

The gray day dimmed and it was night. The wind cried on the desert, sweeping from the valley of great rocks to the cliffs of the mesa. Over the miles they drove on. . . .

Suddenly a flame shot into the dark—higher and higher into the windy night. They stopped, and in the silence they heard only the crying of the wind. . . .

"Chindi," whispered the boy.

Silently they watched the flame of the burning hogan tear the edge of night. They watched it until it sank again, and the dark closed in.

Again it was night. And from the north the black wind blew.